HOLY CITY

By

MP Murphy

This book is a work of fiction. Names, characters, places and incidents are products of the author's imagination or are used fictitiously. Any resemblance to actual events or locales is entirely coincidental.

ISBN-13: 0692247122
ISBN-10: 9780692247129

First Gaslight Books Edition 2014
First North South Publishing Edition 2016

Manufactured in the United States of America by North South Publishing.

Printed in Charleston, South Carolina

For information regarding special discounts on bulk purchases, please contact North South Publishing, or go to www.northsouthpublishing.com.

Front cover Knights of the Golden Circle medallion photo courtesy of the National Archives.

HOLY CITY

Prologue

Liverpool, England
March 25, 1865

"The fall of the Confederacy is almost certain now." James Trenholm addressed a group of three men in a small upstairs office of his father's business, Fraser, Trenholm & Company. "I have received word from Father that Richmond will fall within the week and President Jefferson has begun making evacuation plans."

"Is the company prepared for this? We have a lot vested in the Confederate cause and surely there will be repercussions for our involvement." The gentleman who spoke was the last Fraser to sit on the board. The war years had not been kind to him or his family back in South Carolina. For certain he had very little left to lose.

"We have been making the proper arrangements throughout the war. Currently, here in England and back in the States, plans are in the works that will secure our company." James Trenholm glanced towards a young English gentleman at the end of the table. "Lord Wallace has guaranteed us protection by the crown if the Union decides to punish our international interest. For this reason, we have moved the securities of Fraser, Trenholm & Company from Charleston to Liverpool. All that has been left in South Carolina is the office where we will negotiate cotton prices and shipping orders after the war."

"And what about your father?" The elder Fraser asked still fearful.

"Father's role as Secretary of the Treasury for the Confederacy has left him in a position to secure the funds still owed to us by the government in Richmond. When the city evacuates so will the Confederate Treasury, and with it all the remaining gold and silver coins, bars, and bricks stored in the bank vaults there. He has gotten an agreement from President Jefferson that the treasure will be split with half sent to Charleston and the other half to Savannah, where it will be loaded onto the company's blockade runners and sent on to England."

"That is not my only concern." The old man said. "What of your Father's well-being? Will he not be prosecuted for his role in our government?"

"Between our connections here in England and Father's back in the states, it appears that he will be allowed to return to Charleston after the war. He is fearful that the Union will hold him briefly but is certain it will only be temporary. Many others in his position are already setting up President Jefferson to take the brunt of the Union repercussions against the Confederate Government."

"You seem pretty confident about the fall of the Confederacy and the security of this company." The final man in the room spoke. Dressed in Confederate grey, the man was an associate of James' from Charleston but not a friend. Edward Tidwell was the Confederate attaché to England and a constant problem. "Both Charleston and Savannah have surrendered to

Union troops and are currently occupied. How do you expect to load the remains of the Confederate Treasury onto ships and escape from two Union occupied cities, as well as avoid the Union Naval blockade?"

"Points outside each city have been chosen where the wealth of the Confederacy can be loaded onto flat boats and then sent down stream to where our blockade runners lay hidden and in wait. With the fall of almost all of the South's ports the Union blockade is weak, losing ships everyday as they move into the occupied harbors."

"What locations have you found that Union troops won't discover? Ships being loaded to sail are quite noticeable." Tidwell said suspiciously.

"Those locations are none of your concern. Besides, I am not even sure which locations Father has chosen. I am certain he will rely on the advice of the captains of his blockade runners to decide on the best spots to load the ships."

"I'm sure he has it all figured out," Tidwell said.

"If that is all," Lord Wallace got up from his seat in the room, "I must return to the night's festivities before I am missed. James, I trust everything is in good hands."

The rest of the men rose as well and headed towards the door of the office. Tidwell turned back towards James before he exited. "I am a little uneasy with the fact the Confederate Government is entrusting one family with all of its wealth. It would be a shame to see the whole cause go down because of someone else's greed."

"This family and this company have always supported the Confederate cause and the fight for states' rights, and we always will," James said as he shut the door on Tidwell halting any further conversation he may attempt.

CHAPTER 1

It was a spring day unlike any I had seen before. First, it was still March, and the grass was green, flowers were blooming, and the sun was shining bright overhead, an unusual occurrence for someone raised in Cleveland, Ohio. Besides the 75 degree temperatures, it was also a day of celebration. I arrived in Charleston only the day before to attend the wedding of my closest cousin to his South Carolina-born bride. I never liked to miss a wedding, especially one in such a beautiful town.

I had set myself up in a rented carriage house off of Church Street in the oldest section of the city. The main house was a beautiful colonial built in the familiar Charleston single house style. Its red brick and double piazzas were highlighted by a grand live oak in the garden, dripping with Spanish moss. I sat on the small porch attached to the carriage house and sipped the rest of my morning coffee as I slowly donned my tuxedo for the early afternoon wedding ceremony. It was a beautiful setting, and I was already thinking about staying on a little longer than I had originally planned.

The ceremony was a couple blocks from where I was staying at Saint Michaels Church. From my porch, I could see its white steeple gleaming in the sunlight, and was happy to see a skyline that lacked the obtrusiveness of any modern buildings. Bryce had been one of my closest cousins, even though I had him by quite a few years. I spent a lot of time with him back in Cleveland after his father died battling cancer. Eventually, he left the frozen North to come to school at the College of Charleston, where he met his future bride. Sarah seemed to be a nice enough young woman, but I had not had a chance really to get to know her yet. She came from an old Charleston family with roots going back before the American Revolution, something she was very proud of.

My bowtie was a little crooked, so I took a moment to get it right in the mirror before I went to the small kitchen to rinse out my coffee cup. Outside the carriage house, on a drive paved in Charleston brick, I stood for a moment to soak up the sun and adjust the sleeves on my tux. Mrs. Legare (pronounced Le·gree), the woman I was renting the carriage house from, sat on the first-floor piazza of the main house with a group of ladies having tea. I gave them a wave and a smile as I walked toward the street. They returned it with waves, big smiles, and then a few whispers when they thought I wasn't looking. I am sure the news of a single man renting from Mrs. Legare spread quickly throughout the neighborhood. Each time I walked the drive there seemed to be new faces on the porch, most always women.

I walked north on Church Street and cut down St. Michael's Alley over to Meeting Street and to the front entrance of Saint Michael's Church. A group was gathering out front, and I recognized a few faces as I approached. Bryce's mother Joyce was there to greet me.

"He's inside waiting for you." She said grabbing my arm and leading me inside.

"Is everything all right?" I asked because of the nervous tone of her voice.

"Oh heavens yes. I'm just at my wits' end trying to coordinate our side of the family. Now go and do your duty." I felt a push on my back as she sent me through a doorway and then turned to go back out front.

Inside, Bryce stood in front of a mirror putting the finishing touches on his tux. Next to him was a young man about his age whom I had yet to meet.

"Jack," Bryce said turning towards me, "I would like you to meet my other groomsmen, a friend from college and one of Sarah's good friends growing up. Jack Francis this is Jason Trenholm."

"Please to meet you," I said shaking the kid's hand.

"Same here. Bryce has had a lot to say about his favorite cousin from up North."

"Only good I hope."

"Yes, only good."

Suddenly there was a knock on the door, and the three of us were being called upon to make our way to the front of the church. A beautiful day for a celebration.

CHAPTER 2

The ceremony was short and charmingly appropriate for the colonial church. The bride looked magnificent, and the new couple's love seemed to radiate out into the crowd. From the tranquility of the ceremony came the loud and joyful reception. Drinks were very abundant, including healthy portions of bourbon, and the South Carolina barbecue was almost as good as the Lowcountry oysters. The entire reception was held in the backyard and gardens of Sarah's grandmother's home on the Charleston Battery. The home was nothing less than a mansion, with three story piazzas, a pair of exterior buildings, and spectacular views of the harbor and Fort Sumter. As darkness began to fall, and the chandeliers hanging from the live oak trees came alive, the party took on a rowdiness found only when a young couple gets married. With the music playing, people dancing, and the drinks flowing I became lost in my surroundings and the magic of the whole scene.

I woke the next morning with a blistering headache and a knock on my door. When I slowly rose to answer it, I found Mrs. Legare without her regular Southern genteel composure. The vivacious older woman was now stark white in the face and appeared frantic.

"Good morning," I said with a dry throat.

"Mr. Francis, there is someone here to see you, and it is very urgent."

"Who is it?"

"Not relevant at the moment. You simply need to dress and come up to the house quickly."

"Give me a moment, and I'll be right up." The woman turned and scampered back up the drive in a hurry. I took a quick glance at the first-floor piazza and saw no one waiting for me. Odd, considering that was Mrs. Legare's normal meeting spot.

I rinsed the smell of booze off of me with a quick cold shower and threw on a pair of shorts with a light button down from Brooks Brothers. I covered my tired eyes with a pair of sunglasses and splashed on some cologne before I ventured out into the morning sun. When I made it to Mrs. Legare's door, she was there to greet me and quickly ushered me into the first-floor study, where I was greeted by a concerned looking Bryce and an older gentleman I did not recognize.

"Mr. Francis," Mrs. Legare said, "I'd like to introduce you to Mr. George Trenholm."

"Pleased to meet you." I gave the man a firm shake.

"I'll leave you gentleman be." Mrs. Legare said as she retreated from the room.

George Trenholm took the chance to move behind the desk in the room and sat down. Bryce followed suit by moving to the sofa, and I took it as a clue to sit myself in a chair facing Mr. Trenholm and the desk.

"What is it that I can do for you, Mr. Trenholm?"

"Please, you can call me George."

"All right George."

"Jack, if I may, last night something terrible happened to my family. Shortly after the festivities ended for Bryce and Sarah, my son, Jason, was found murdered in Stoll's Alley, apparently on his way home from the reception."

"My God, I'm so sorry." I gave a quick look to Bryce, who appeared near tears.

"Thank you. Bryce here tells me that you were once in the FBI and are currently still in the business from a private aspect."

"Yes, I was with the Bureau for ten years. Now I do security consulting and some private investigation work. But I have taken a break from work for nearly six months now."

"Well, I am hoping then that you will be willing to get back into it. The murder of my son, I assure you, has already spread across this town. However, more delicate matters may come about because of it. I would like to hire you to investigate why and who killed my son and bring me any information you find first."

"I'm not about to willingly involve myself in a cover-up of some kind if that's what you're asking?"

"Not at all, I'm quite certain Jason's reputation will go untarnished. It is the family I'm more concerned about."

"I believe I've heard this request before," I said, thinking back to Captain Gilmore in Cleveland.

"Jack, as an outsider let me explain to you a little bit about Charleston. Even though it has become a modern city, it is still very much a small Southern town. Those of us whose families have been here since the beginning have rebelled against England, built fortunes from slavery, and tried to secede from the Union. During this city's long history families have intermarried, bonds formed and bonds broken, secrets made, and secrets kept all for the benefit of keeping the family wealth and promoting what we believe in. There are a lot of people out there that are loyal to the Trenholm family, but there are just as many in this town that would love nothing more than to see us destroyed. All I am asking is for you to stay on top of the investigation and keep me informed, so that I may act and react according to what you find."

"What you are telling me is someone killed your son, and you believe they are out to destroy you family too?"

"I'm not saying for sure, but there is a good chance there is more here than simply murdering Jason. No one randomly gets killed walking the streets South of Broad, so there must be more to it."

"You seem very confident, George. Any reason you can give me as to why?"

"Not willingly. Are you prepared to accept my offer, Jack? I can promise you it will be worth your while."

I looked over to Bryce sitting quietly on the couch. His eyes pleaded me to say yes. "I will help you. Jason was a good friend to Bryce, and for that alone, I would help."

"Thank you. Our family will forever be grateful." George Trenholm said, with a face that was only slightly more relieved.

CHAPTER 3

In a room in the attic of a Victorian home in the Cannonborough neighborhood of Charleston, a man was slumped over a desk. The room behind him was shabby and humbly furnished. A twin bed sat unmade, a dresser unpainted, and a TV about twenty years old was on in the background with the sound turned down. Spread across the desk was an array of papers containing land records, family trees, and property holdings. The man looked haggard, but a fire shone in his eyes. He drank too much coffee and ate too little. On the wall above the desk hung his most prized possession, a Confederate sword that looked as clean and well-kept as the day it was made.

The man got up from the desk and walked over to a small table that held a coffee maker. The pot was empty, and he prepared a fresh one as he watched the news on the television. As he waited for the coffee to brew, he turned up the volume on the TV and sat on the bed to watch. The news of Jason Trenholm's murder in the historic and wealthy South of Broad neighborhood had shocked the city. East Bay Street and the Battery were covered in about as many journalists as tourists, each one gawking and straining for a look or a word from someone with information. The whole scene intrigued the man.

Once, a long time ago he was destined to join the privileged ranks of the Charleston aristocracy that live in the South of Broad neighborhood. His family had the necessary link to the founding of the city, participated in the War for Independence, owned plantations, and supported the Confederacy, but since then it had all disappeared. The legacy tarnished, and the fortunes withered away to nothing. Nothing now could ever place him back in the upper-class. His family name had fallen too far, and in a city with a long memory and love of history it would remain that way forever. There were incidents when the citizens of Charleston could forgive, but they would never forget.

With his coffee done the man once again turned the TV down. He poured himself a fresh cup and returned to the desk. He stared at the papers he had been poring over for days and finally looked up at the sword above him. Any time he began to lose his sense of determination, the need for retribution and felt tired with his life the sword reminded him of whom he was and why he was here. It gave his life meaning and a passion to follow. He knew very well that life was nothing without passion so he would continue with his work and his family duty. Unexpectedly, today he needed the sword to remind him once again. He was surprised that he did not feel more driven. Instead, he felt drained knowing he had a lot of work still to do.

The man took the sword off the wall and grabbed a polishing cloth from the desk drawer. He rubbed the sword down gently, tracing its details, and the superior craftsmanship. Toward the base of the blade, he was careful to work around the name carved into the steel. Expertly scrolled with a master's touch was the name of the man's great-great-grandfather, Edward Tidwell.

CHAPTER 4

George Trenholm excused himself, and Bryce and I made our way to back to the porch of my carriage house. I still hadn't had my morning coffee, so I put on a pot and started frying some eggs, as Bryce sat down at the kitchen table. He was quiet, and eyes seemed to stare off to nowhere. Yesterday was one of the most joyous of his young life, and today was a striking opposite. He and Sarah had planned to leave tomorrow for their honeymoon, but now I was getting the feeling those plans were going to be put on hold.

"Are you all right?" I asked, setting breakfast and coffee down in front of him.

"I'll be okay. I'm just in shock still I guess."

"You want to talk about him? Sometimes it helps."

"Yes, but not yet. I'll fill you in on Jason later."

"I didn't mean for the case. I only wanted to talk. It might help with how you're feeling."

"Oh, no I'm okay for now. Like I said, still in shock."

I watched as Bryce fumbled with his eggs for a moment before getting up and reaching in the fridge for some hot sauce. The South was already having a positive effect on the young man. He swallowed down his meal in silence, and I did the same. The effects of last night's reception were wearing off, and I was beginning to feel a little closer to my usual self.

"I'm going to go," Bryce said getting up and putting his plate in the sink. "I need to find Sarah. I'm sure she's a wreck with all this."

"It makes sense. It looks like I'll be in town for a while, so if you need me, I'll be here."

"Thanks. If you want to get started on your work for Mr. Trenholm, you ought to start with Dr. Welsh over at the college."

"Why's that?"

"Dr. Welsh was Jason's graduate advisor. They have been spending a lot of time together doing some kind of research. I'm not sure what exactly. I've been a little distant from Jason these last couple months with Sarah and all the wedding planning. I guess I'm starting to regret it now."

"Don't," I interjected. The last thing I wanted was the kid to get down on himself.

"Well, anyways he was spending all his free time working on something." Bryce went for the door.

"Thanks for the help, and don't forget I'm here if you need me.

"You always are. Dinner tonight?"

"I wouldn't miss it."

"Great, I'll call you later."

I watched as Bryce headed down the drive towards Church Street with his head down, unaware of the world around him. For me, it was time to get ready to go to work, something I hadn't done in months, and part of me was actually looking forward to. Too bad it was under the worst of circumstances.

CHAPTER 5

The campus of the College of Charleston was small and as beautiful as the city it was in. A vast canopy of ancient oaks covered me as I crossed the Cistern Yard to the administration building. Once it was made known that I was working for Mr. Trenholm, I was whisked by golf cart over to Dr. Welsh's office. The Doctor was a Professor of Southern History at Columbia and had come down to Charleston to do research for a new book. The College of Charleston was happy to have the distinguished Columbia scholar, who was also using the opportunity to teach a few classes on campus.

I was shocked when I knocked on the Professor's office door to hear a woman's voice beckon me in. Apparently, I am a sexist who was unable to conceive that a notable Columbia professor, with a doctorate in Southern History, could be a woman. I am glad I was mistaken.

Dr. Welsh was roughly my height, with straight brown hair and the most beautiful cheekbones. She was dressed in a skirt that was cut below her knees and wore a billowy top very well. There was a pair of glasses resting on her head and to my surprise appeared way too young to be a professor.

"What can I do for you?" She asked moving around the desk to shake my hand.

"Dr. Welsh, I am Jack Francis," I said shaking back. "I am here working for George Trenholm, Jason's father."

"Oh, certainly. Sit. What can I do for you and Mr. Trenholm?" She asked moving back behind her desk and taking a seat herself.

"By your tone, I am going to have to assume you are not in touch with the local gossip today?"

"Not at all. I got to the office early today. I like to start off Mondays early so I can leave early when Friday comes."

"Then you haven't heard?"

"Heard what?"

I didn't want to be the bearer of bad news to a woman I just met, but it looked like I had no choice. "Jason Trenholm is dead." There was no easy way to say it.

"What? How can it be?"

"He was apparently murdered last night walking home from a wedding reception."

"Bryce's?"

"Yeah."

"He had been talking about it for a while now. Jason was really excited for Bryce and Sarah. Actually, that was all he was talking about on Friday while we were working."

"Dr. Welsh, if it is not too much trouble can I ask you a few questions about Jason? Mr. Trenholm has asked me to look further into the matter for him."

"How did that come about?"

"Bryce is my cousin, and he knew I was formerly with the FBI, so he recommended my services to Mr. Trenholm. If you don't want to talk now, I will understand."

"No, it's fine. Some people close up when they are upset. Me, I'm more of a talker. What do you want to know?"

"Honestly, I'm not sure exactly. Typical information, like what were the two of you working on? Did any of his routines change recently? Any new acquaintances? Stuff like that."

"As far as Jason's routines, nothing appeared to change. And I don't see him outside of our research work so I can't really answer about his acquaintances. You see, I didn't get to know Jason socially."

"Okay, Dr. Welsh, what about your work together?"

"Please call me Hannah. I came down to work on a book about the role of Charleston's businessmen in the black market during the Civil War. The college allowed me an office and access to their resources in exchange for my services as a guest lecturer. When I was interviewing graduate assistants Jason's name stood out because of Fraser, Trenholm, & Company, a major player here and in Europe during the War Between the States. They were major financiers for the Confederacy, as well as owning a large amount of the South's blockade runners. Jason's name, and the fact that his grades and references were superb were all I needed to bring him on to the project."

"If I might ask, what exactly where the two of you researching?"

"Records from local companies, family documents, land deeds, and other historical evidence we could find. The idea was to paint a picture of the scope of the black market here and in the rest of the South, as well as understand how much money was being made by the men who ran the trade."

"I know this is an old town with a lot of old families. I met a lot of them at the wedding. Could your research be upsetting to any of the old money here in town?

"I'm sure it could be, but I felt the Trenholms were in a position to be the most upset, and I assumed we had their blessing since Jason was on the project."

"Why would the Trenholms be the most upset?"

Hannah looked at me like I was an idiot and maybe I was. "The Trenholms were in control of Fraser, Trenholm & Company during the war, which made them a fortune from the trade their blockade runners brought in and took out of Charleston Harbor. It was also rumored they paid off members of the Union government so they could keep their wealth and property after the war, even though Jason's great-great-great-grandfather was Secretary of the Treasury for the Confederacy."

I was beginning to see the issues Hannah and Jason's research could dig up here in Charleston. I couldn't believe it was enough motivation for murder, but then again less-trivial issues had been motive enough in the past, and these Southerners were still sensitive about the war.

CHAPTER 6

I left Hannah's office with a lot more questions than answers, and as I moved down the bustling King Street shopping district. I knew I had to look further into the Trenholm family's past. King Street was packed full of designer stores, local eateries, and tourists who were looking everywhere but where they were going. It seemed like every five feet I had to dodge someone with their head turned in the wrong direction. Eventually, my odds were going to turn against me, so I wasn't surprised when a man struck me right in the shoulder as he passed by.

"Hey!" I yelled out when he struck me. I am not a Southerner nor do I pretend to be, so I wasn't going to apologize because somebody else wasn't watching where they were going. The man kept walking right past me, only turning his head slightly back and giving me a glimpse of his venomous smile. He was definitely no tourist.

I moved on down the street finally cutting across Queen and over to Church Street where the crowds were gone, and I had the sidewalk to myself. The man who bumped into me had left a lasting image with the way he looked back, almost as if he knew me and certainly like he ran into me on purpose. It was something

I did not want to be focusing on at the moment, knowing I had bigger things to worry about.

Mrs. Legare was sitting on her first-floor piazza with a large pitcher of tea when I made my way to the driveway. "Why don't you join me?" She said waving me up.

"I would love to. Do you mind if we talk a little bit about a few things?"

"I do love to talk, but mind your manners."

I understood what she meant. She was warning me not to be too pushy with the conversation. The Southern way of conversation was far different from what I had been raised with. Up North, we are more direct and straight to the point, but in Charleston that kind of behavior would make you an outcast.

"How has your day been?" I asked as I sat down.

"Oh, quite lovely all things considered. You look parched may I?" She asked hinting at the pitcher on the table beside her.

"I think I will."

As she poured, I could smell the fresh mint she had placed in the glass and prepared my pallet for the sweetness of the tea. When she handed me the glass, to my surprise, it smelled more like bourbon than tea. I took a small sip and then smiled at the woman.

"Aren't mint juleps such a lovely drink?" She said.

"And they look like iced tea from a distance."

"Don't I know that?" She smiled at me with a mischievous grin. "Now what have you been up to today?"

"I walked up to the college to talk to the professor, a Dr. Welsh."

"I'm not sure if I recognize the name, must not be local."

"No, in fact, she is down from Columbia University to do some research. Bryce had told me that Jason had been working with her, as her graduate assistant."

"Really, whatever were they working on?"

"A little Charleston history."

"Well, there is nothing I like more than Charleston history. In fact, I like to consider myself a resident scholar on the subject. You know my family has been around this city since the beginning."

From my short time in Charleston, I have learned a couple things. No one is shy to tell you how long their family has been in the city, and no one loves their own history more than Charlestonians.

"That's good to know, because you may be able to help me to better understand what Jason and Dr. Welsh were working on."

"Oh, this sounds fun. What do you need to know? I am sure I'll know all about it."

"Apparently, Dr. Welsh and Jason were working on a little Trenholm family history. What do you know about Jason's ancestors, especially the ones during the Civil War?"

CHAPTER 7

"The Trenholm family has a fascinating history, one long up for debate." Mrs. Legare started. She paused to top off my drink as if to say settle in for my tale. "The story you are probably looking to hear begins with George Alfred Trenholm, who I believe would have been Jason's great-great-grandfather or something close. Anyway, George left school at a young age, after his father passed away, to work at Fraser & Company, a cotton broker here in town. Before long George rose through the ranks and became head of the company, eventually attaching his own name to the moniker. Some people here in town believed he forced the Frasers out of their own business, but the reality of it was he expanded the firm from cotton to slaves, plantations, steamships, hotels, and banking."

"So that's how the family got their fortune?"

"The first time."

"What do you mean the first time?" I asked.

"When the War for Southern Independence broke out Fraser, Trenholm & Company became the overseas bankers for the Confederacy, which gave them direct access to the government in Richmond and international markets. They financed armaments through the trade of their own cotton, tobacco, and turpentine. The company also funded blockade running, the construction of Confederate warships in England, and they became the unofficial ambassadors for the Confederacy in Europe. By the end of the war, the Confederate Government was heavily indebted to Fraser, Trenholm, & Company."

"Let me get this straight. The Trenholm family sacrificed their own wealth and that of their business for the Southern cause."

Mrs. Legare laughed. "No such thing ever occurred. The Trenholms made another fortune off of the war, through trade and blockade running. George Trenholm would never have done anything unless there was a profit in it."

"Well, then that's how they made their second fortune."

"No, the money the Trenholms took in during the war was just added on top of what they already had. To make a second fortune, you would have to lose the first."

I was beginning to believe the woman was enjoying telling this story more than I was listening to it. "Let me guess the loss of one fortune and the acquirement of the second is the real tale?"

"I'm not sure if it's a factual story, but it is definitely a good one. You see this is where the Trenholm family history is up for debate by us Charlestonians. You see, near the end of the war George went to Richmond to become Secretary of the Confederate Treasury, a good position for him considering his personal success. However, most people were upset because it put all of the Confederate finances in the hands of one family. The gold and silver in the Treasury, the debts they owed, and all the tax collecting were now in the hands of the Trenholms, who already represented Confederate banking in Europe."

"A pretty powerful place to be in, except you said the war was almost over, wasn't the Confederacy broke?"

"To continue a full-scale war, yes they were broke, but that doesn't mean the Treasury was empty. In fact, the truth was the exact opposite, and most people knew it. The Confederate Government had been selling cotton to Mexico in order to build up treasury funds. It was rumored that the banks in Richmond held a considerable amount for the government to access."

"I'm beginning to see the problem with George Trenholm as treasurer. The Confederacy owed his company a substantial amount, and now he held the debt and the way to pay it off. The man could allocate the funds to pay off what was owed to him and ignore the Confederacy's other needs."

"That's correct."

"But I still don't understand how he lost his fortune then," I said a bit confused.

"The war ended."

CHAPTER 8

"The war ended?" I asked. "What did that have to do with anything? It seems to me that the Trenholms were in a pretty good position to survive past the war."

"They were, except George Trenholm was a traitor for participating in the Confederate Government as its treasurer. When the Confederacy surrendered, everything was taken from him, and he spent some time as a prisoner in Fort Pulaski down near Savannah."

"I guess that makes sense, but I would have thought a man like George Trenholm would have had prepared for such a thing."

"Some say he did. Within a year of being released from Federal captivity, he was as wealthy as ever."

"How did that happen?"

"This is where the story becomes more rumor than truth. The answer could be simple, like the possibility that the Trenholms had deposited a vast amount of their wealth into foreign banks to protect it after the war. But the story most Charlestonians like to tell is a little more sinister."

"My kind of story."

"When Richmond was about to fall to Grant's forces, President Jefferson Davis made evacuation plans for the capital. These designs included George Trenholm and the National Treasury. The Confederate Government, with the Treasury in hand, retreated south until they reached the Carolina backcountry. It was there that Trenholm split from the rest of Davis' party and headed back to Charleston."

"It seems reasonable with the war at its end," I interjected.

"Yes, very reasonable, but the question is who took the gold and silver held in the treasury, President Davis or Trenholm?"

"Shouldn't that be a matter of record?"

"No there was no record and the fact remains that the gold and silver in the Confederate Treasury were never recovered after the war."

"What you're telling me is that many people believe Trenholm took the money back to Charleston with him to pay off debts owed to him by the Confederacy and then used the money to support himself after his own fortune was confiscated by the Federal Government after Appomattox?"

"I'm not telling you that, it is simply what some people believe." Mrs. Legare looked very pleased with her storytelling as she capped off our drinks from the pitcher. "The story goes that the money was split up into two parties. One was to head to

Savannah where it was to be loaded onto a blockade runner and then sent to England. The other party was to head to Charleston with the same intentions. The idea was to send the money to Europe where it could be kept safe until the Confederacy could once again fight for their cause. The problem with this story is that both Savannah and Charleston were occupied by Union troops, and the blockade runners in both cities were owned by Fraser, Trenholm & Company."

"What you're having me believe is that the Confederate treasure has been missing since the end of the Civil War and that all signs point to the Trenholm family as the number one suspect in its disappearance."

"Oh, my heavens, I would never suggest the Trenholms had anything to do with it, they are such a lovely group of people. All I am telling you is a story, in which many in this town believe has some truth to it."

"Of course, it is simply a little Charleston tale you wanted me to hear." *This city and their manners*, I thought.

"Exactly."

"You don't suppose this was what Jason and Dr. Welsh might have been looking into. I mean, wouldn't have Jason known all about this?"

"I'm sure Jason knew about the story I told you, but I doubt many in the Trenholm family know the truth. The fact may be that no one knows the truth anymore. I am sure Jason was just as intrigued by the story as anyone else in this town."

"I guess then that it is a real possibility."

"I would think so, but you should ask Dr. Welsh to be a little more specific next time you talk to her."

"I plan on it." I hadn't gotten into details with her before because of the shock of Jason's death, but I really liked the angle even though I wasn't sure how it connected to Jason's killing. "Thank you for the mint julep," I said sitting down my glass and standing from my chair.

"Going so soon?"

"I have to get ready for dinner with Bryce. Thank you for talking to me. It was very informative."

"If you ever need some more information you know where to find me." Mrs. Legare said with a smile.

I had no doubts that if I needed a tidbit of town gossip I could find it very quickly on Mrs. Legare's piazza.

CHAPTER 9

We had dinner at Cypress, a new southern restaurant on East Bay Street. Once the wine had been finished, the check paid, and Sarah and her family departed back to their South of Broad home, Bryce and I headed back to my carriage house on Church Street for a little family bonding time. I could tell he was ready to talk from the way he excused himself from his new wife after dinner. She seemed to understand.

It was a beautiful night, so we poured ourselves a cocktail and grabbed some cigars at the house before returning to the Charleston streets. Church Street was quiet with the sidewalks illuminated by gas lamps and ancient trees dripping with Spanish moss overhead. We walked in silence for a while, smoking our cigars and taking in the evening. It was Bryce who finally broke the silence.

"Did you get a chance to talk to Dr. Welsh?"

"Sure did and boy was I surprised to find out she was a beautiful woman. Unfortunately, she hadn't heard about Jason yet when I showed up at her office."

"You had to tell her then?"

"I did, but she was strong and still talked to me for a bit."

"Sorry," Bryce said. "I wouldn't have sent you over there if I had known. The way news spreads in this town I figured she would have heard the minute she opened her front door."

"Don't worry about it. It wasn't the first bad news I've had to deliver in my time. How are you holding up?"

"I've been better, but I'll survive. Sarah's taking it harder than me."

"I think you've got yourself a good one there. Make sure you take care of her."

"Thanks." Bryce grew silent again as we reached White Point Gardens, a park at the end of the Charleston Peninsula. We walked over to the battery wall and stared out over the harbor. "You know I've been thinking a little." Bryce continued. "There is something else you may want to look into." Jason was a pretty perfect guy, close enough anyway, but he did have one fault."

"Oh yeah, what's that?"

"He had a little passion for sports betting. Nothing I ever thought was a problem, especially since we all did once in a while. But in the past year, he went from using an internet site to going to a bookie. He told me it was because the odds were better and he could get his cash faster…made sense."

"With the internet taking over every aspect of life even the bookies have to change their style to compete. Do you know his guy's name?"

"Yeah," Bryce began. "Tommy Makem. I'm not sure if it's anything, but it's the only thing I could think of at the moment."

"You never know what you'll find. It could be nothing, or it might lead to something more. Any little bit of information, no matter how unimportant it may seem, could help to find out who killed Jason. Do you have any idea where I could track down this Tommy Makem?"

"Jason always met him at the Cocktail Club on Upper King Street."

"The pre-prohibition cocktail bar?"

"That's the one."

"Not exactly the kind of place I would expect to find a bookie."

"From what I've gathered from Jason, Tommy 's not really your stereotypical bookie."

"Well, that could be something too. Either way, I'll check it out tomorrow. It's getting late let me walk you back to your bride before she starts to worry about you."

"I can make it on my own," Bryce said. "We're staying with her parents right down the street."

"Normally I would let you go, but not tonight. I'll sleep better knowing you got back to your bride safe and sound."

"All right," Bryce conceded. He turned from the battery wall and began to head back through the park. I took one last look at the water and followed behind him.

CHAPTER 10

The next morning, I put a call into my former partner at the FBI, Special Agent Colin Sommers, to see if he had any information on Tommy Makem. Though the FBI's system is fast, I hardly rated top priority and would probably wait most of the afternoon for any news. The only lead I had to follow at the moment was the one Hannah Welsh had given me, and Mrs. Legare backed up. I figured it was about time I saw Professor Welsh again for a little history lesson.

I met Hannah at the South Carolina Historical Society on a long break she had between lectures. The building was constructed as the first fire-proof structure in the United States and was filled to the brim with old documents containing the State of South Carolina's colorful history. I paid my dues with a slight donation upon entering and then found Hannah hunched over some papers at a quiet table.

"How's the work coming?" I asked her, as I approached the table.

"Fine, but tortoise slow. Jason usually came down here to do the grunt work, so I'm not used to where everything in the building is yet."

"Maybe I shouldn't be interrupting you then."

"No, it's quite all right. You're here to ask about the work anyways, so actually it fits nicely." Hannah moved some papers around and motioned me to sit next to her. "Come on sit, and I'll give you some of the details if it doesn't bore you too much."

"Not at all. I got the neighborhood gossip version from Mrs. Legare yesterday and found it very intriguing."

"I'm sure her story was a bit more colorful than what I am working on."

"I have found that the truth is always much more interesting than fiction." God knows my years at the Bureau had proven that. "What are you working on today?"

"Well, the idea of the research is to paint a picture of the families who participated in the black market, either through blockade running or trading, before the war. I want to gather financial information to determine a general grasp on the value of the family estates."

"Where does Jason's family fit in with this?" I asked, already having a good idea.

"Right at the top. George Trenholm built a vast empire through the slave market, plantation production, and shipping. In fact, he may have been the richest man in Charleston, and one of the richest in the country before the war started."

"Ok, you've got the background on the main families involved in black market activities during the war, so what's the next step?"

"That's where it gets tricky, and as a researcher, I need to dig a little deeper and do some interpretation of the documents available to me," Hannah explained. "Learning about a family's fortune before the war was easy because many kept detailed account books for their business and personal wealth and the South Carolina Historical Society now has possession of many of them. During the war records on blockade running and illegal trade weren't kept in open documents, so I have to dig through personal journals, diaries, letters, and other paperwork to determine a general picture of a person's business activities. Comparing one's daily journal from before the war to that of journals during the war can tell you a lot about their lifestyle change as well."

"That sounds incredibly time-consuming."

"You have no idea."

"How far along were you and Jason in your research?" I asked, generally interested.

"Honestly, pretty far. I hadn't started writing my book yet, but the research was mostly done. All we had was a few holes to seal up before I could reach my conclusion."

"And what might that be?"

"I'm not exactly positive how I'm going to write a conclusion to my work yet. The holes we had left to fill could change a lot about the way I view my research."

"What were conclusions on Jason's family?"

"You see Jack, therein lies the problem. The Trenholm family history is where I'm trying to fill most of my holes."

"I don't understand. You had Jason, didn't he have access to his own family history?

"Sure he knew his family history from what his father and grandfather told him, but what he was told and what we were beginning to find started to contradict each other."

"Let me ask you something about the Trenholms that I got from Mrs. Legare's story. It's not based on research like your work, but instead merely town gossip."

"Okay, I'll bite."

"Have you come across any connection between the Trenholms and some lost Confederate treasure."

"Jack, you're about to grasp where my holes are coming from."

CHAPTER 11

"Through our research, Jason and I were able to trace the path of financial wealth for most of the families involved. When people find dire straits, or accumulate vast sums of money, they are very likely to write it down in their own journals, but George Trenholm wasn't like everyone else."

"What do you mean?" I asked Hannah.

"First, there are very few primary sources on the Trenholm family."

"What do you mean by primary sources?"

"Personal letters, diaries, journals, objects of that nature. Most of the old Charleston families have donated these types of documents to the Historical Society, the Preservation Society, or the college to establish their role in the history of the city and the nation for that matter. The Trenholms have given very little, and practically nothing compared to other families of the same standing. The one important piece we do have access to is George Trenholm's journal from his time in Richmond, and for the most part, it tells us virtually nothing. The man either wrote with microscopic detail or chose to leave out a lot of his life."

"The holes you are trying to fill then come from the Trenholm family history during the war."

"From the business side of the family, yes. From a personal side, we have nothing before, during, or after the conflict."

It was definitely curious to me that the Trenholms decided to not follow the rest of the old families in the city in donating their ancestors' documents to the city's history, but that wasn't enough to make Mrs. Legare's story real. "How do these missing documents connect the Trenholms to the lost Confederate treasure?"

"There are subtle clues," Hannah answered. "For example in the final pages of George Trenholm's journal from Richmond, he does mention the issue of the Treasury and the questions President Jefferson, and he, had in transporting the vast sums out of the city. Secondly, his son James, who worked for the family business during the war in England, notes in the company ledger next to the Confederate debts owed that his father was handling them."

"That could mean anything."

"It sure could, but remember when working with so little we must connect the dots as best we can and interpret the history for ourselves."

"But doesn't that close your mind to other options?"

"No, the idea is to interpret history from every angle and study all the options. It gives the researcher a better perspective on the subject being considered and the decisions being made at the time."

"It still doesn't explain how you connected a note in a ledger from England to the Confederate treasure. You've got to have something better?" I asked doubtfully.

"I do." Hannah pulled a folder from her bag next to her chair and opened it on the table. Inside was a timeworn letter, aged yellow, with a precise cursive hand. "This is a letter Jason discovered in the family library. It was actually in an old copy of *The Republic* by Plato."

"A simple question of the just and unjust and how it applies to government and human character." I knew a little about the work.

"Precisely, but a simple question with a complicated answer."

"Does Plato's work apply to the letter Jason found?"

"I'm not sure. The letter appears to be a simple communication from a father to a son, George to James. However, there are a few things that stand out. The first is the date and where the letter is addressed." Hannah moved closer to me and pointed to the top of the page. "If you look here the letter is dated April 26, 1865. That date is important for two reasons."

"The day John Wilkes Booth was shot in a barn and dies," I interjected, wanting to show off my knowledge.

"Yes, that is one. The other reason is that James was still in England on that date, but the letter was sent to the home in Charleston."

"Maybe his father didn't know."

"Possibly, but doubtful. They were in constant contact because James was in control of the company's interests overseas.

44

James also didn't return to South Carolina until September of 1866. So the letter wasn't written in hopes that he would be home soon.

"Okay, I'll give you that. It makes Booth's death more of a coincidence than the letter being sent to James in Charleston."

"I agree," Hannah said. "The other thing that really stood out to me is this." She turned the letter over to the back and on the top right corner there was a small marking.

"What is that?" I asked. It didn't look like anything more than mere scratches of a quill.

"Jack, that is a hooked x, a symbol often associated with the Knights Templar and even the Masons. It has been found on archeological sites from Rosslyn Chapel in Scotland to the often-disputed Kensington Runestone in Minnesota."

"So what connection does it have with Jason's family or his death?"

"I'm not exactly sure. As a scholar, I've written off the hooked x as nothing more than a conspiracy theory reserved for the History Channel, but having found it on a document from

1865 makes me curious. I've had the letter examined by a couple of my colleagues, and it appears to be legit."

"I believe this whole case is quickly becoming out of my league. Missing Confederate gold and now Masonic symbols, I'm pretty sure my FBI training didn't prepare me for this."

"Well, I've got something else you may relate to a little easier then," Hannah said. "The marking was originally written in invisible ink."

"They had invisible ink during the Civil War?

"Invisible ink goes back to the Romans and Greeks in natural forms, and the Colonists used it often during the American Revolution. It's a relatively straightforward spy tactic, but an effective one."

"The question remains, what is the marking doing on the letter?"

Hannah looked over the letter, flipping it from back to front and front to back a few times. "I'm still not sure. The body of the document seems pretty straightforward and legitimate, but the hooked x, the date, and the fact that it was sent to someone who wasn't there to receive it all add up to too many coincidences for me."

"Do you think the body of the letter is coded in some form?" I asked.

"I do, except I haven't been able to figure out how or why?"

CHAPTER 12

"Yeah, what is it?" I awoke to the phone ringing next to my bed the next morning.

"Good morning, and rise and shine sleepy head." I heard Colin's voice come from the other end. "Rough night last night?"

"Not really, just a long couple of days. How are things in Cleveland?"

"The wife's great, the weather sucks, and work is a bore. You know the same old thing. I've meant to ask you if you plan on coming home anytime soon. With spring right around the corner, I thought maybe I could get your car out of winter storage for you."

I had left the care of my beloved Austin Healy in Colin's hands when I had left town last fall. Since then, I've found myself traveling warmer climates. "I don't know when I'm coming back and you can pull the car out of storage, but only when the last snow has fallen up there. I don't want a single bit of the salt they use to clear the streets touching my baby."

"Fine, I guess I'll wait till April then."

"Good idea. Was the car the only thing you were calling about, or do you have a better reason for waking me up?"

"It's after eight, you should be up anyway."

"Who says?"

"Whatever. I'm calling because I have the information you asked for on one Tommy Makem."

"And?"

"He's clean. No record and we don't even have a file on him. I even went out of my way to call Atlanta to see if they had something on the guy…nothing. The only thing I found was that his father was Sean Makem."

"Sounds familiar," I said trying to clear the morning fog from my brain.

"It should. Sean Makem had connections to the Celtic Club and Danny Greene."

"Wasn't Danny Greene the Irish mobster who became an informant for the FBI?"

"Sure was. Greene helped bring down the Italians here in Cleveland. Of course, they ended up killing him with a car bomb soon afterward."

"Other than his dad's connection to the Irish mob, what does this have to do with Tommy?"

"Nothing, but I thought you would like to know the kid's back story before you go sticking your nose where it probably doesn't belong. Forgive me for helping you."

"Sorry, I'm still half asleep."

"Must have really been a rough night?"

"I told you it wasn't. I'm just worn out."

"Do you need me to take a few days off and come down there? You know, to give you a hand." Colin asked hopefully. "I hear the weather is beautiful in Charleston this time of year."

"I'll be okay, and there is no need for you to waste vacation days helping me work a case."

"I wasn't coming down for help, only moral support."

"I think I'm good on that," I said.

"Oh really?" Colin asked inquisitively.

"Yeah, there is Bryce and his family here to give me support."

"Who's the lady?"

"I'm not sure I get what you're asking."

"With you, there is always a woman," Colin almost snickered.

"Not sure what you mean. I've got to go, and thanks for the help." I quickly hung up on him before another word could be said, and then I gave myself a smile.

I heard the shower turn off and Hannah stepped out of the bathroom. "Do you want to grab some breakfast before my first class?" Hannah asked as she dried off her hair.

"Definitely." I got out of bed and quickly threw on some clothes. From the window, I could see Mrs. Legare and a couple of women having coffee on the piazza. "The gossip mill will be running today," I said, pointing to the ladies.

"Oh, I can't wait to make their day. I'll hurry and get dressed, so we don't miss them on the way out." Hannah quickened her pace, and I had to laugh at her relaxed attitude.

CHAPTER 13

After breakfast Hannah and I had gone our separate ways, she had classes to teach, and I had plans to meet Bryce and Sarah at her parents' Sullivan's Island beach house. What could have been a relaxing day of lunch on the oceanfront porch turned into an uncomfortable afternoon. Sarah was still a complete wreck over Jason's death, as I'm sure Bryce was, but he held firm in order to support his new wife. Tensions were running high with everything that happened over the past couple days, and a day at the beach was no day at the beach. Most of the afternoon was spent discussing sensitive subjects and avoiding Sarah's tears.

That afternoon I decided to have a little happy hour at the Cocktail Club in hopes of meeting up with Tommy Makem. The bar was in the trendy Upper King Street District and sat on the second story of a historic building. The building had been stripped down during the remodeling to expose the beams on the ceiling and between each room. The effect was interesting, as it left the bar feeling open, but still providing different areas for socializing. The drinks were pricey and took a while to make, but the end result was something truly delicious.

I finished up my first cocktail as a man walked up the stairs and into the bar. He sat at the last stool at the end and immediately chatted up the beautiful brunette tending bar. He was comfortable in the place and an obvious regular.

Noticing my fluids were running low, the bartending headed my way. "Another round?" She asked.

"Yes…please." In the five minutes, it took her to make my cocktail I began to wonder if the man could be Tommy Makem. He did not have the appearance of a bookie, at least not one from where I grew up, but he did have an aura about him that you wouldn't find from an average business man. His clothes were cut nice, probably tailored, and he was well-groomed, but underneath there was an aggressive nature that belonged to a man who did a lot of fighting to get to where he was.

"Here you are." The bartender said as she set my drink down. "Anything else at the moment?"

"Actually there is. Who is the man at the end of the bar?"

"You mean Mr. Makem? He's one of our regulars. Comes in Monday thru Friday around this time, but we never see him on the weekends. The crowd in here changes then, and the regulars always hide until Monday comes again. Anything else?"

"No thanks, I think I'm okay for now."

I waited a few minutes sipping my drink about half way down before I took it with me and sat next to Mr. Makem.

"Can I help you?" He asked a little annoyed with the breach of his personal space.

"Are you Tommy Makem?"

"Yeah, who's asking?"

"Jack Francis. I was wondering if you wouldn't mind talking with me about a few things?"

"About what?"

"Jason Trenholm."

"I was wondering when this conversation was going to happen, but you don't seem to be one of the local guys."

"I'm not. I'm actually from your hometown."

Tommy almost looked pleased by the fact. "Well, another Clevelander. Okay let's talk, and if the conversation turns sour, we can always move on and talk about the Browns."

"Another sour topic."

"No doubt."

CHAPTER 14

"Jocelyn, can we get another round down here?" Makem called out to the bartender.

"Sure thing."

"I think I'm going to switch it up a bit. Do you have any Pappy Van Winkle?" The pre-prohibition cocktail I had been drinking was good, but the mood called for a little bourbon.

"12, 15, 20, or 23 years old?" Jocelyn called back.

"The 15 year should do the trick."

"Nonsense pour the man a 20-year-old and put it on my tab." Makem offered.

"Thanks."

"From one Ohio boy to another. Now let's talk about Jason. I've got nothing to hide, so do you want to ask the questions or should I just start talking."

"Whatever you're more comfortable with."

"How about I talk and you sit there and sip on your bourbon. If you have any questions, we can work them out when the time comes."

"Sounds fine with me."

"Jason came to me about three months ago," Makem began. "He contacted me through a mutual friend."

"Does he have a name?"

"Her name is Sarah, and that's all I'll give you."

I almost choked on the name Sarah. Must have been a coincidence, but then again there are no coincidences.

"So Sarah set Jason up with me," Makem began again. "He wanted to bet the ponies and some college football. Generally, I take a small deposit from new clients, but Jason came from good stock and was well backed, so I looked the other way. The kid lost a good amount of money testing the waters of college basketball and March Madness, but since then he was playing the horses very well."

"Did he owe you anything?"

"I was getting to that. Isn't that always the question when somebody shows up dead? Jason owed me some money, but not to the point where I was worried. Like I said, he was doing well with the ponies, and he was well backed." Makem pulled out his phone and played for a minute. "According to my records, the kid only owed me 5 grand."

I almost spit out my bourbon. "5 grand seems like a lot."

"Not really, not for these old Charleston families. They have plenty of money, and besides Jason had owed me more a month earlier. When he was losing, it was closer to 15 grand. The kid paid his dues, so I wasn't worried. If I were getting nervous about his debt, killing him would not be worth the $5,000 I would be out."

"Seems like a good point to me." I could tell Tommy Makem was being sweet, giving me the story without much of a fight. Either the man was telling the truth or he wanted me off the track. "Was Jason betting with any other bookie that you know of?"

"Nah, if he were then I might have a reason to kill him." Makem laughed and gave me a smack on the back. "I'm the only game in town for someone willing to bet real money."

"Any other ideas as to why Jason may have been killed?"

"Not that I can think of, but then again we only had a business relationship. We would chat here over a couple of drinks, but like I said that was business. Maybe you should ask Jocelyn here. If there is one thing, I know, it's that the bartenders in this town have all the decent gossip."

What was it with Charleston and gossip? "I might just do that, but not today. I need to let some things sink in first. Tommy, you're not leaving town on vacation anytime soon, are you?"

"Not at all, I'll be right here if you need me." He patted his big palms on the bar top.

"Thanks for talking with me, and thanks for the Pappy," I said tossing back the last of my drink. Tommy Makem seemed innocent enough, but I knew better. His type never left anything to chance, when it came to saving their own asses.

CHAPTER 15

My phone rang. It was 3 A.M.

The first time I ignored it, the second time I woke up a little pissed. "What?" I half-yelled into the phone.

"Jack, it's George Trenholm. Throw some clothes on and get over here fast something has happened."

"What is it?"

"Never mind that just get over here."

"Fine, but I don't know where you live."

"16 Meeting Street, someone will be there to meet you." The man hung up as promptly as he called.

I took my time getting dressed and even made some coffee. I've had enough middle of the night phone calls to know I wasn't going back to bed anytime soon. I knew from the address that the Trenholm residence was not that far away, so I stepped out onto the dark Charleston streets and began my walk south towards the end of the peninsula.

16 Meeting Street was not a house, nor could it be called a home. I was pretty sure by the sight of it that it was the biggest house in Charleston, an amazing feat in a city filled with magnificent homes. The house was fenced in and the grounds concealed from the street, but as Mr. Trenholm suggested someone was waiting for me at the gate.

"Good morning," I said to the man, and with as much enthusiasm as I could muster.

"Good morning Mr. Francis. Please follow me." With no introduction, the man led me through the front gardens and into the house.

Inside I was greeted by a grand entranceway, complete with Italian tiled floor and a large chandelier. The house was split down the middle by a large hall, decorated with three more chandeliers and an array of heirloom antiques. I followed the man into the hallway and was quickly ushered into the first doorway on the right. The man did not follow but instead showed me the way with an opened door and the wave of his hand.

"Mr. Trenholm will be right with you. Please have a seat." Once again with no introduction the man closed the door and left me alone in the great house.

I found myself in the library, or entirely possible Mr. Trenholm's study. The walls were covered with antiquated books, and a large oriental rug covered the floor. Above the fireplace was a massive gold leafed mirror, and in front of the only window sat a Victorian desk, big enough to serve dinner on.

"Please have a seat, Jack," George Trenholm said from behind me as he came into the room.

I took one last look around the space then placed myself in one of the two chairs directly in front of the desk. Trenholm moved behind it and took a seat in the leather chair. "What's so important that it couldn't wait until morning?" I asked.

"We had a break in tonight."

"Really, the house looks calm and in one piece to me."

"It wasn't your typical break in. Someone knew how to get in the house without setting off the alarms, and they came looking for something particular."

"How do you know?"

"The house alarms didn't go off, but I have a second security system to guard my office. There are sensitive company documents stored in this room, so it needs a little more protection. The alarms in this room went off this evening and woke me up."

"Did you see who broke in?" I asked, still not convinced the break-in was worth waking me up in the middle of the night.

"No, we didn't get his face. It was a man, but Johnson lost him in the shadows after chasing him down the street for a few blocks."

"Johnson?"

"He's the gentleman who showed you in."

"Oh," I said, wondering how that relationship worked. "You mentioned that the thief was after something specific, how do you know that? Is anything missing?"

"Let me put it as delicately as possible. This house is filled with an immense fortune worth of art, antiques, jewelry, and other valuable objects. There is enough in this room alone to make the average burglar euphoric, but none of that was touched tonight. Whoever that man was, he was here looking for something specific."

"Okay, I see your point. You still didn't tell me if anything was missing."

"Nothing obvious, but I haven't had time to look through everything."

"Why don't you go through everything a call me after the sun comes up with the results?"

"I've got a better idea, why don't you sit tight here while I go through my things. That way you can start the investigation into this break-in a lot sooner."

"You hired me to look into your son's murder, not to chase down petty criminals."

George Trenholm sneered at me then covered it up quickly. "I would bet my soul that the two are connected. Now sit tight. I'll have Johnson bring in some breakfast and coffee. You can fill your stomach will I go through my office."

"Fine."

CHAPTER 16

I was wiping my last bit of biscuit through some grits when Trenholm finally spoke to me. The man had gone through his desk, an obvious safe, a safe hidden behind a painting, a secret compartment built into the desk, and finally moved onto the bookshelves when he apparently found something.

"I found what the thief must have been after."

"What's that?" I answered as I swallowed the last of my food.

"An old letter from my great-great-grandfather to his son." He said, turning around and holding an opened copy of Plato's *The Republic*. "I should have known." I heard the man mumble to himself.

"I can imagine why a letter like that is important to you, but why would someone want to steal such a thing?" I had no intention of telling him that I knew where the letter was until I got to hear more about it.

Trenholm froze on my question for a second and then quickly recovered. "I can't imagine why. Though there are some history buffs out there that would find anything written by my ancestor valuable."

"Why is that?"

"Because of my namesake, George Alfred Trenholm was Secretary of the Treasury for the Confederacy, and we all know how radical some historical groups can be."

"It's an angle," I said, pretending to think on it. "Is there anything else about the letter, anything in its contents that someone may find valuable?"

"I doubt it. The letter is simply a communication between father and son."

"Then why do you believe this break-in was connected to Jason's murder?"

The man froze for a moment caught up in his own antics. "Well…maybe I jumped the gun on that connection."

"Or there is something you're not telling me. How can I help you or your family if you don't tell me everything you know, and every reason someone may have wanted Jason killed?"

"I don't know why someone would want the letter." The man was near yelling and defiant. "I do know someone broke into my home to steal it mere days after my son was killed. How can they not be connected? Now Mr. Francis, are you going to help me retrieve my letter and find out who murdered my son, or am I going to have to hire someone else?"

"I have no intention of doing anything but solving your son's murder, and if it leads me to your letter...well then...we all win."

Trenholm grew quiet and took a seat behind his desk again. He pulled out a drawer and began to write. "Here you go." He said as he ripped a check from his checkbook and handed it to me. "This is to start, and I'll double it if you find my son's killer and my letter."

"I'll do my best." I took the check and tucked it into my pocket. "I guess I'll be getting started then." With that, I turned for the door and left the man sitting behind his desk. In the hall, Johnson was there to escort me to the front door. "Nice to meet you, Johnson," I said as I stepped into the garden. The only sound I heard in return was the heavy door closing behind me.

CHAPTER 17

I had two things I knew I needed to address. The connection between Sarah and Tommy Makem had me thinking. It could be nothing, and maybe all of these blueblood children had too much dispensable income to spend on extracurricular activities, but Sarah knowing a bookie seemed odd to me. The second thing was whether or not to tell Hannah about George Trenholm and the letter she was in possession of. There was a chance that if I told her he thought it had been stolen she would want immediately to return it and explain the situation. Because the man was apparently keeping information from me, I didn't want that to happen. On the other hand, I may tell and she might do the opposite. Hannah was a researcher on a mission, and that letter was the key to her work…and possibly mine. If the letter went back to the Trenholm residence, neither of us would ever see it again.

The morning air was a little crisp as I walked down Broad St. to a small French café to meet Hannah. Breakfast was some strong French pressed coffee, cheese, ham, and some fresh baked bread. An assortment of mustards and jellies complimented the meal. Hannah had arrived first and had the spread ordered and waiting when I arrived. She was buried in a manila folder when I sat down next to her.

"Too early for you?" she asked as she set down the folder.

"I was up earlier yesterday." I figured I would tell her about the letter and try to convince her to keep it if I had to. "George Trenholm woke me up before the sun had risen claiming his house was broken into. Apparently, the alarm in his office went off, and his butler chased the perp down the street only to lose him."

"Seriously, what was stolen?"

"Nothing, but Trenholm seems to think a particular letter is missing from his copy of Plato's *Republic*."

"Shit. Are you serious?"

"Sure am. Now don't jump the gun and go running it right over to Trenholm. He hasn't called the police, and in my personal opinion he's hiding something."

"Like what?" Hannah asked obviously concerned about the whole situation.

"I'm not sure yet, but the man has been real vague with my questions. Especially for someone trying to find his son's killer. It's my hunch that if we return the letter to him, neither one of us will see it again."

"That does leave me in a predicament. I guess the letter isn't technically stolen since Jason gave it to me. Plus, I really think it holds some clue to my research."

"Mr. Trenholm isn't reporting the letter stolen to the police, so technically it hasn't been taken, and unless he asks you personally if you have it…well then there is no way you would know that he is looking for it. I'd say you're safe to keep it."

"You said that someone did break in though?" Hannah asked with a little concern in her voice.

"According to Trenholm, his butler chased the man down the street."

"So what was the intruder after? Could he have been looking for the letter since nothing else was touched?"

"I guess I haven't thought about that. As Trenholm pointed out, the house is filled with valuable items and nothing else was touched. It might be a safe assumption that the letter could have been what the man was after, but how did he even know it existed?"

"I'm not sure since Jason didn't even know about it until recently."

"Hannah, I would keep that letter out of sight and well-hidden until we can find out a little more."

CHAPTER 18

Four of us sat on the porch of the carriage house I had been renting. I had finished dinner with Bryce and Sarah at a pizza joint in the Park Circle neighborhood called EVO. Now I sat with the two of them and was joined by Hannah for some after dinner cocktails and a little brainstorming. It might have been spring, but the wind coming off of the Cooper River and blowing through the old historic streets had a chill to it. I could hear the branches of oak and magnolia trees clack together as each burst passed through their leaves. A half-moon showed bright through a partially cloudy sky as the gaslights flickered on the porch. It was chilly enough that we were all having our drinks stiff and iceless.

The three of them were already sitting comfortably. Sarah and Bryce were under a light blanket on the porch swing when I came out with a bottle of rye and four glasses. I poured for everyone and then made myself comfortable.

"Who wants to be a storyteller?" I asked the group.

"What story are we telling?" Bryce asked.

"Good question. Let's start with a little Trenholm family history, so Sarah or Hannah should take this one."

"You probably should go down to the main house and get Mrs. Legare," Sarah said. "She fancies herself a local historian."

"I already have gotten her story of the events. Hannah why don't you give me what you and Jason were working on in a little more depth? I really believe Mr. Trenholm has been hiding a few things from me."

"Okay, where should I start?"

"How about you tell me about George Alfred Trenholm and the end of the war."

"I see," Hannah said. "Well, George Alfred Trenholm was one of the most prominent men in the Confederacy. From his role as the war's premier operator of blockade runners to his position as Secretary of the Treasury, his actions had more influence on the Confederacy and its ability to fight a war than most generals and politicians. During the war, his firm, Fraser, Trenholm & Co., made significant contributions to the Confederate war effort. It acted as the private overseas banker of the Confederate Government and financed the supply of armaments, gunpowder and other essential goods in return for cotton, tobacco, and turpentine. The company also participated in blockade running, had vessels built for the Confederate Navy, assisted in the floating of Confederate loans, and encouraged support in Europe for the South. By war's end, the organization controlled over sixty large steamers and numerous sailing ships which operated out of Charleston, Savannah, and Wilmington. Trenholm's successful blockade running ventures made him both wealthy and powerful. On July 18, 1864, he replaced Christopher G. Memminger as Secretary of the Treasury in President Davis's Cabinet. As skilled as he was with money, Trenholm couldn't rescue the Confederate economy. After the fall of Richmond, he took flight southward with the rest of the Cabinet, but in ill health, was unable to continue running, so when the party reached the

South Carolina upcountry Trenholm split from Jefferson Davis and returned to Charleston."

"When Trenholm left Richmond with Davis, did they take the Confederate Treasury reserves with them?" I asked Hannah.

"There is some documentation to believe that they did, and common sense tells you that they wouldn't leave it for the approaching Union Army, so I think they did have it with them."

"So it's possible Trenholm could have taken it with him when he split from Davis and headed to Charleston?"

"Yes, it's possible," Hannah said matter-of-factly. "There is also the fact that no sign of the Confederate treasure was found with Davis, which means Trenholm did take it or Davis abandoned the heavy load somewhere else along his journey."

"What happened when Trenholm came back to Charleston?" Bryce asked. "Weren't the Union troops waiting for him…the city was occupied."

"Yes, he was taken by the Union authorities upon his return. They sent him down to Fort Pulaski near Savannah."

Sarah finally spoke for the first time. "There was a rumor in Charleston lore that was slightly different."

"What's that?" I asked anxiously.

"Well, local residents always believed that Trenholm stopped outside of town on his way back. Trenholm knew once he returned to Charleston that he would face prison. It was also alleged that Trenholm was traveling in ill-health. Any stay in Fort Pulaski would probably kill him in his condition, so his party stopped outside of town while he rested."

"Jason mentioned that to me as well," Hannah said. "But he never knew where."

"I don't think anyone does for sure," Sarah said. "The story is that he stayed at a couple different plantations, moving to avoid Union capture until his health returned."

"It sounds like the man had time to stash a treasure then," I said. "Whether it was aboard a hidden blockade runner or at one of the plantations there was definitely an opportunity if Sarah's story is true."

"Oh, it's not my story, just a little Charleston history that missed the books."

"I don't know how all of this history plays a part in Jason's murder, but the Trenholm family seems to get more mysterious every day. And so far, it appears to be the best lead other than Tommy Makem." I gave Sarah a quick glance, but she didn't even blink at the bookie's name.

CHAPTER 19

The man observed the gathering, a benefit for some useless charity put on by the wealthy to make themselves feel better. *I hope it works* the man thought as he watched a group of men dressed in dinner jackets talk about the weekend hunting trip. A sneer showed across the man's face as he dreamt about following them out to their stately plantation and hunting each one down...now that would be a hunting trip to remember.

His focus tonight was not on the men, but a group of woman, chardonnay in hand, gathered and pecking like hens around the silent auction merchandise. Earlier in the afternoon, he had found the perfect hiding spot among an unkempt corner of the backyard garden. The shrubbery, in need of a trim, concealed and old iron gate that led to an alley. The lane at one time had been used for servant access to the stately old mansions along the street. The man now crouched spying on the rich from a vantage point they had once created with their own desire never to see those that served them, and now it was serving him well.

One woman, in particular, held his gaze, which was impressive because they all looked alike. Three hundred years of inbreeding amongst Charleston's wealthy had left most of the current generation looking like the distant cousins they probably were. There was also the "keeping up with the Jones" effect where each woman shopped, got their hair done, and sent their kids off to the same school as all their neighbors. The man grimaced at the offensive nature of their lives. These women had no desire in life except to marry rich and keep the bloodlines of the old families alive. Hell, they didn't even raise their own children that was done by the nanny. He would be doing this world a favor by cutting down a few of them in the prime of their lives…soccer moms more spoiled than their kids, if that was possible.

The woman he watched now ventured to the first-floor portico of the old home and dug through a purse. A cell phone appeared at her ear a second later. She spoke for a moment and then put the phone back in her purse where she dug for something else. The man smiled to himself as he watched. *Our impeccable South of Broad housewife has a nasty habit,* he thought following the woman as she walked towards the front of the house with a lighter and cigarette in hand.

The man got up from his crouching stance and looked one last time at the party. *Little do these people know that with their arrogance they have created their own nemesis.* And with that last thought, he made his way down the alley back towards the street. He had seen enough tonight to know it was time for him to make his move. What a pleasure this night would be.

CHAPTER 20

I had taken a liking to the little French café that I had met Hannah at and decided to grab another breakfast there. I ordered a coffee and grabbed a paper from the stack at the end of the counter to keep myself occupied until my food arrived. The article was previously read, and I had to comb through the pages to reorganize and find the front page. To my shock, the headlines read *Another South of Broad Murder* as bold and as loud as they could. I quickly scanned through the article.

The woman had been found hanging from the trees in White Point Garden like an angel descending from the heavens, naked and painted white. The police weren't giving much information, but apparently, the reporter had seen the body before they closed off the crime scene. It was being rumored that the body belonged to a divorced mother of two. It appears that she lived in her ex-husband's ancestral home in the neighborhood. A family tradition apparently stated that the female heir must reside in the house and the woman's daughter was that heir. So, the husband moves out, and the ex-wife stays because she has custody. *Wacky town*, I thought.

It was obvious that the husband would be looked at first because he definitely had a motive, but I had a hunch he was the wrong person. I pulled my phone out of my pocket and texted Hannah just as my food arrived. She hadn't known about Jason's death when I first met her, so I figured she hadn't seen the paper yet this morning. I was wrong.

Within minutes, I had my food down and the check paid. I was out the door and down the street heading towards campus faster than I ever thought I could. Hannah had apparently seen the paper, and her first thought was that the husband was innocent as well. I made it to her office so fast that my head was beginning to dampen with sweat as I sat down in front of her desk partly out of breath.

"Whatcha got?" I asked.

"It may be nothing…did you run here?" She asked.

"Fast walk after wolfing down breakfast and scalding coffee in record time."

"Oh, you look terrible."

"Thanks, so what do you have?"

"It may be nothing," She started again, "but we may have a connection between today's murder and Jason."

"Really?"

"I'll need to look into it further, and I'll have to wait for the police to confirm the victim, but Jason was related to today's victim."

"I'd say that's something."

"Could be, but in this town, all the old money is related somehow."

"My thought was that these two murders were related, but I'm not sure why…just a hunch. Jason's was made to look like a mugging gone bad, but apparently, the killer spent more time with this victim."

Hannah thought for a moment. "Do you feel it was done that way so the police wouldn't connect the two?"

Possibly, or maybe Jason wasn't supposed to die in that alley or like that.

"What do you mean?"

"What if the killer wanted to kidnap Jason, interrogate him, and then take him somewhere else to leave the body? What if the plan went awry somehow?

Once again Hannah was silent for a moment as she thought everything through. "That could make sense. The killer could have wanted to interrogate Jason in order to learn the location of the letter, which someone is obviously after because of the break in at the Trenholm house."

"Exactly. There's a lot of maybe in this theory, but it definitely has some traction. We will definitely need to confirm the name of the victim in White Point this morning before we can look into it further. Once we do, how much history do you have on the Trenholms outside of Jason's direct line?"

"Just about everything that has been made public over the years."

"Okay, I'll leave the research to you then. If we are going with the connection between the Trenholms and the lost

Confederate Treasury gold then we will need to know how our newest victim plays into it."

"I can handle that," Hannah said. "What's your next move?"

"I have the inevitable task of speaking to my cousin's new wife about her gambling habits."

"That should go over well," Hannah said with a smile.

CHAPTER 21

Sarah was a frail woman to begin with, but she had a resilient set of baby blue eyes that told a person she was stronger than she appeared. When I met her and Bryce for lunch at SNOB, a go-to lunch spot for the locals and tourists, she was dressed in jeans with a pair of knee-high brown leather boots and sporting a Barbour vest on top of her shirt. Bryce pulled out the chair for his young bride as they sat. Sarah's face told that the news of the morning's murder blocks from her family home was taking its toll.

We started lunch off with some small talk desperately trying to avoid any type of upsetting conversation. I think everyone knew that this wasn't a typical lunch call, but I wanted to wait until the food was down before I started to ask any awkward questions. The restaurant was known for its local fare, and Bryce ordered shrimp and grits accordingly. Sarah settled for the beef carpaccio and a bowl of She Crab Soup, and I stayed small with the charcuterie plate and a generous helping of Kentucky rye.

I didn't know quite how to start a conversation with my cousin's new bride, so I jumped right into the big question hoping I wouldn't have to apologize too much later.

"Sarah," I began, "Do you know a man by the name of Tommy Makem here in town?"

Bryce sat calm and unresponsive as Sarah gave me a small smile. "Tommy is a bookie my friends and I have used over the years."

Initially, I thought that this line of questioning would set off some embarrassment, but the girl was unapologetic. "How did you come to meet Tommy?" I asked.

"I met him through Daddy. He would come by every Saturday morning before the Gamecocks played to let Daddy place his bets. Over the years, we would also see him during poker nights the men in the neighborhood would have in our carriage house, so he became a familiar face to me."

"Did you place any wagers with him?"

"Occasionally when we would be planning for a big event like the Kentucky Derby just so I would have a stake in the race but nothing serious. Most of the time I would only point my guy friends at school towards Tommy when they were looking for a little action."

"So that's how Jason got involved with him?"

"Yes," Sarah answered. A little sadness came to her blue eyes at the mention of Jason's name. "Jason was wasting his money betting online. Had I known earlier that he was such the gambler I would have introduced the two sooner. I was really surprised when he didn't already know Tommy, but his father wasn't one to gamble or even attend the neighborhood card game."

"You're saying Mr. Trenholm didn't socialize much with the rest of the neighborhood?"

"Not unless he had to. There are certain gatherings you cannot say no to." Sarah informed me as if this was obvious.

"You said Jason was a big gambler…"

"I believe I said he was such a gambler." Sarah pointed out.

"Sorry. What did you mean by that?"

"He was wagering serious money when I found out he was using internet sites to lay down bets."

"What type of money do you consider serious?"

"Well," Sarah thought for a moment, "he had one account credited with ten-grand and another with five, but that's all I was aware of."

"That is some serious money for a kid his age. Did he still use those accounts after you introduced him to Tommy?"

"Not as far as I know of," Sarah said.

"No, he didn't," Bryce interjected for the first time. "He told me that he cashed those out and moved all of his credit back into his checking account. He had a particular checking account set up for any frivolous activities he wanted to partake in."

"I see." It was nice that Bryce was helping and not upset with my line of questioning. Apparently, they both must have known it was coming since Bryce pointed me to Tommy Makem in the first place. "Can either of you tell me what Tommy is like when you owe him money? Have you heard of anything violent ever happening to someone?"

They both shook their heads no before Sarah finally spoke.

"He's been known to show up at places that might embarrass you, like sitting behind you at church or during a business lunch, but I've never heard of him getting violent. Most of his clientele has money to cover their debts. And if they don't have, someone in their family does."

"So neither of you would suspect Tommy Makem might come after Jason for a gambling debt?

"I don't think so," Sarah said. "Jason's dad had plenty of money to cover any debts, but then again so did Jason."

Bryce sat quietly staring at his plate.

"What do you think Bryce?" I asked.

"Probably not, but Jason's dad hated gambling and would have been furious if he knew his son enjoyed it, let alone had a bookie. I could see Mr. Trenholm refusing to pay any gambling debts out of principle. I don't think Tommy has had anyone deny him before, so I'm not sure what he would do."

And there it was, the moment of doubt. I was almost able to check Tommy Makem off my list of suspects, and Bryce hands me a shred of doubt. Mr. Trenholm did seem to be the man Bryce had described, one who would refuse to pay off a bookie. He would refuse to pay out of principle, but also because he felt a man like Tommy Makem was below him. I, on the other hand, knew people like Tommy from the Cleveland FBI, and my experience with the history of the Italian and Irish mafias in that town's East and West sides. Men like Tommy go after debts owed to them, whether the fish is big or small. I needed to look into Tommy a bit further if I was going to clear him and focus my time on other leads.

CHAPTER 22

The peacefulness of the Charleston nights is a welcome relief from the chaotic tourist infested days, and as I walked home from dinner under the shadows cast by the gas-lit street lamps I could only feel relaxed. I was happy, full, and content even with all that was happening in my life. But the moment I turned up Church Street it was all shattered in an instant.

The lights from the police cars flickered and ricocheted off of the windows on the skinny street. I picked up my pace and as I made my way closer I knew they were coming from Mrs. Legare's house. Between the FBI and being a private investigator, I had been around enough to know that police late at night in a generally safe neighborhood was never good, and right now I feared the worse. The only spot of hope was the fact that there was no sign of an ambulance anywhere, or was that because the coroner was called instead?

It took me a few minutes to get through to one of the local cops that I was staying in Mrs. Legare's carriage house. My Ohio ID hadn't helped my argument either, but once I was able to get my point across to the young black and white I was able to go on towards the home. When I hit the drive, I could see Mrs. Legare speaking with a pair of officers on her piazza, and I was instantly relieved. But what could have happened to bring on this much attention from the Charleston Police Department?

I stood in the drive for a few moments and took in the scene while I waited to approach my temporary landlord. She eventually waved me over. The officers turned to look as I approached.

"Jack," Mrs. Legare started, "this is Officers Jackson and Smythe.

"What happened?" I asked.

"The carriage house was broken into."

"Really?" I was honestly surprised knowing I had nothing of value in there, and also knowing that the main house was filled with valuable antiques. "Do we know who it was?"

"Not yet." Officer Jackson stated. "Mrs. Legare came to let her dog out one last time before bed when she saw the man coming out."

"I tried to stop him." She interjected. "But he pushed me to the ground. Can you believe that? Who pushes an old woman like myself?"

"Anyway," Officer Jackson continued, "Mrs. Legare was lucky he didn't hurt her. Her screaming and yelling alerted the neighbors and the man took off."

"What did he look like?" I asked Mrs. Legare directly.

"Like a tour guide."

"What do you mean?"

"You know he was dressed like a tour guide. He wore Confederate garb, but not very well, and he was unkempt."

"Unkempt?" I asked looking for more details.

"He was unshaven and just seemed dirty."

"Did you get a good look at his face?" Officer Jackson asked.

"No. It was dark, and he wore an old Confederate hat, just like the tour guides. Besides, it happened so fast, and my eyesight is not what it used to be."

"Why would anyone be dressed in an old Confederate outfit to break into a house?" Officer Jackson wondered out loud.

"I told you he looked like one of those tour guides. They are always around here late at night on those ghost tours. He was probably on a tour earlier and thought no one was home, so he came back to break into the house."

It wasn't a bad theory, and I'm sure Mrs. Legare had been working on it ever since the break in. For a city that survived on tourism the locals, like Mrs. Legare didn't care a whole lot for outsiders' intrusion, which is why her mind went there first. But my mind instantly went somewhere else. The Old Confederacy appeared too often for me lately, and I couldn't take this as a simple burglary. The first reason was that it was evident that I was targeted and not the antiquated wealth of Mrs. Legare's house. Second, when I'm on a case and I, or someone I know, gets unwanted attention, it's never a coincidence. And third, the Confederate garb on the intruder was simply too odd...even in Charleston.

CHAPTER 23

"The letter," I said into the phone hurriedly. "Is it safe?"

"I have it right here," Hannah responded. "I've been working on it all night trying to figure out whatever message it may have hidden. Why?"

"Someone broke into the carriage house I'm staying in. I could only assume they were after the letter."

"The same person that broke into Mr. Trenholm's study."

"That's what I was thinking too. It appears that you weren't the only one that was able to grasp the importance of that piece of paper."

"I haven't grasped anything yet," Hannah exclaimed. "This piece of paper still hasn't given up its mystery to me. I do have something else for you, though."

"Oh yeah, what's that?"

"Eliza Dunn was confirmed as the victim in the White Point Garden murder, just as the neighborhood gossip told us. It was on the local news tonight."

"And how was she related to Jason again?" I asked.

"They were distant cousins, but I don't believe that's really as important as something else I found."

"I can't imagine. Go on then."

"Eliza may have been a distant cousin to Jason, but she was a direct descendant to Charles Fraser, who was the final member of his family to sit on the board of Fraser, Trenholm & Company."

"So both Jason and Eliza are connected because their ancestors were in a position to profit from the disappearance of the Confederate Treasury?"

"Exactly, Jason is a direct descendent of George A. Trenholm through his eldest son James, who eventually took over the business and Eliza through Charles Fraser. Both James Trenholm and Charles Fraser appeared to have been in England during the Fall of Richmond, and had control of the company's assets there with protection from the crown."

"Why haven't the cops put all of this together yet?" I asked.

"Simple, it's because they are not following a conspiracy theory about lost Confederate gold to solve their murders. They still believe Jason's death was a mugging gone badly, and right now Eliza's ex-husband is being questioned in her death."

I thought about everything for a moment; the letter, the two killings, and how they all may be connected. "Have you ever heard of the old trick to uncovering invisible ink using iodine vapors?"

"No, why?"

"It's an old spy method we learned at Quantico. It shows where fibers on paper have been previously dampened and reveals any hidden messages, as long as the whole piece of paper hasn't been exposed to too much moisture."

"Okay," Hannah said. "What's your point?"

"I was thinking why not try it with the letter. If the invisible ink was used once, why not to conceal a full communication? The visible message may simply be a decoy, instead of a coded dispatch."

"Jack, you may be part genius. Different types of invisible ink are exposed through various agents. It's possible the hooked x, and the message were written in two separate types of ink. Having a universal agent would really make sense for code cracking but not for code writing."

"Of course if that doesn't work you'll have to go back to the beginning."

"I'll get some iodine tomorrow and cross my fingers. Good night Jack."

"Goodnight, I'll get in touch with you in the morning."

CHAPTER 24

The morning started just as the night had ended. I met with Hannah at the South Carolina Historical Society and quickly discovered that my carriage house had not been the only victim the previous evening.

"It was a mess," Hannah said. "My whole office was trashed. Months of research scattered, student papers were thrown everywhere, and my hard drive was ripped from my computer."

"Whoever it is was getting frustrated." I gathered.

"The good news is your iodine theory worked. I was going to do it here but then thought twice about bringing iodine into a library of historical documents."

"Who knows how many secrets you could expose in here," I said, only half kidding. "What did the iodine vapors present?"

"In between the lines of the letter a separate communication was written in invisible ink, but, unfortunately, that message makes no sense to me. Here have a look for yourself."

I glanced at the page yellowed with age. In between each line of elegantly written script was a series of letters, dots, and numbers scribed in a simpler hand and appeared faded compared to the visible contents of the letter. At first glance, I couldn't make out anything from them, but I knew there was something there.

The messages read:

J.A.M.

Holy light and savior of ships is where they find eternal rest.

"Short and to the point you might say" I handed the letter back to Hannah. "Any ideas?"

"I have a few, but they all require some research. How much time do you have today?"

"I'm all yours until happy hour."

"Why, do you have plans?"

"No, I just don't like to work past happy hour," I said to her with a smile.

"Very well. Let's get to work then, and if you do a good job, I'll let you buy me a drink afterward."

"Sounds good. What do you want me to do?"

"I need you to find any history, in fact, all the history, on prominent burial sites in the city. For now, we will only focus on the places where the wealthy were buried because of the connection to the Trenholms and the hooked x on the letter."

"What's the hooked x have to do with it?" I asked.

"The association of the hooked x is most frequent with Stone Masons and Templars, and neither of those two groups are often associated with being poor."

"Why the burial places of the wealthy?"

"The phrase *eternal rest* usually means a burial place. I could be wrong, but it's a good place to start. Also, burial sites are often connected to churches, which would help interpret the words *holy* and *savior* in the message."

"What about the *J.A.M.*?"

"I have no clue, and it's probably important considering it plays such a predominant role at the top of the code. One step at a time, though. Now go." Hannah said waving me away. "Go find a librarian to help you and don't come back until you've got something."

"What are you going to do?"

"Research, on a few more ideas I have in my head."

CHAPTER 25

A young blonde woman, who I could only assume was a grad student or intern, helped me find the section of the Historical Society I was looking for. She pulled out about half-dozen books that I hoped could give me a little light on the location Hannah and I were hoping to discovery. Most of the time I hated the stale smell of libraries, their dark and dreary corners, and the silence could drive a man insane, but today with the help of the young blonde woman's perfume and the thrill of the chase I was a bit more excited to be there.

The first book I went through was about St. Andrews Episcopal Church on the outskirts of Charleston. Its location to the plantations along the Ashley River gave it the prestige I was looking for in a burial site. It also appeared to be the oldest church in the area and its proximity to the waters of the Ashley River gave me some hope that I would figure out what savior of ships meant in the revealed message. Unfortunately, there was nothing more in the book to give me any certainty that I had found my answer on the first try

I then went on to an old volume on St. James Church in nearby Goose Creek with no luck. There were a few books on family burial plots at area plantations. These were harder to go through because I needed to understand who owned the property, who was buried there, and each plantations' history.

A good portion of my day was wasted going through plantation records. Hannah probably would have told me I was wasting my time, and I was, but these old plantation homes were also burial grounds for the area's aristocratic families. I discovered that patriot Henry Laurens had been buried on his plantation Mepkin. Mepkin Plantation it turned out was now Mepkin Abbey, which struck the holy cord but that was all. I was running into a lot of dead ends and wasting a long part of my day.

Two books were left sitting in front of me as I stretched my arms back behind my head with a yawn. My backed ached from sitting, and I was hungry. I was hoping it was time to break for happy hour, so I checked the clock on my cell phone…still had a good hour and a half. It looked like I had no excuse but to keep pouring through the history of Charleston.

I grabbed the closer of the two antiquated volumes and opened it up to begin the story of St. Phillip's Church, which was just down the street from where I was staying at Mrs. Legare's. Everything was looking like another dead end. There was the typical colonial founding, fire, new church, fire, and then build a new church. I could see the city had a problem with fires. It was a little footnote in the church's history that briefly caught my attention. Apparently, the current church building had been used as part of the lighthouse system to guide ships into Charleston's treacherous harbor. Now I had something. I was sure of it. I continued on and found out that signers of the Declaration of Independence, The Constitution, and even the Father of the Confederacy John C. Calhoun were all buried at St. Phillip's. In a city filled with churches and cemeteries, this one was beginning to feel right.

I picked up the book from the table and quickly stood, anxious to find Hannah and tell her what I found, but before I could even step away from the table, my whole world suddenly became black.

CHAPTER 26

When I came to, the smell of perfume filled my nose before my vision cleared and I could see the blonde-haired grad student shaking me.

"Mr. Francis…Mr. Francis are you okay?" I heard her in my foggy head.

"I think so. What happened?"

"I'm not sure." She said to me. "I found you on the ground unconscious. I was coming to check on you and see if you needed any more help finding additional books, but you were out cold and on the floor."

I thought long and hard about how I ended up on the floor and nothing came to me. I rubbed my eyes clear and began to get some clarity from them. The poor grad student had a sincere look of worry on her face. Sitting up, I tried to organize myself and my thoughts, but when I ran my hands through my hair, I began to get a better sense of what happened. On the back of my head, I felt a lump start to form, and a throbbing pain was beginning to swallow my brain.

"I think someone hit me," I said uncertain at first. "Is there anyone else in here?" I asked.

"Nobody except you and the Professor."

"Hannah!" I exclaimed.

I tried to get to my feet, but my knees buckled on my first attempt and I was saved from falling again by the cute blonde.

"Thanks," I said holding on to her. "I don't think I caught your name."

"Lizzy." She told me with a smile.

"Thanks, Lizzy. Can you help me find Hannah?"

"Sure. The last time I saw Professor Welsh she was going through a collection of diaries in the main reading room. This way."

Lizzy slowly let go of my arm, and I took my hand off her shoulder with a little uneasiness and a bit of a wobble. Slowly I put one foot in front of the other and followed her to where I hoped to find Hannah safe and sound. The trip up the old staircase was a bit rough, but I was able to make it without incident. We passed through the marble-floored lobby and through two large oak doors into the main reading room. Inside, where I initially met Hannah that afternoon, were rows and rows of books. Particles of dust shimmered in the light that passed through the windows, and the air still held the stale smell of decaying paper. Desks with table lamps were placed throughout the room, and I look toward the spot where I had left Hannah hours earlier. The lamp on the desk was on, and a couple leather bound books were spread across its wooden top. I could see Hannah's messenger bag on the floor and her notepad on the desk, but there was no sign of her.

"Hannah!" I called out "Hannah!" I yelled again as the first cry for her name still echoed around the room. "Hannah!" I yelled a third time.

"Don't you know that this is a library?" A voice said behind me.

Lizzy and I both turned to see Hannah standing in the doorway behind us, a smile on her face as she put her hair up into a ponytail.

"Are you all right?"

"As far as I know," Hannah said.

"Where were you?" I asked.

Hannah got a concerned look on her face. "Can't a lady go to the bathroom? What's got you all worked up?"

"I found Mr. Francis on the floor, Professor," Lizzy said. "He thinks someone hit him from behind."

I rubbed the bump on my head for a moment. "Got me pretty good."

"Do you think…?" Hannah began.

"Yeah, that's why I was worried about you. Where's the letter?"

"Right here," Hannah said patting her back pocket. I don't go anywhere without it."

"It might be a good thing this time, but next time it might get you hurt. Whoever it is that came after me must have missed you…barely."

"Lucky me."

"Yeah," I said rubbing my head again.

"I'm going to grab you some ice, Mr. Francis."

"Thanks, Lizzy." The young woman made her way out of the room. Hannah went over to the desk she had been working at and began to gather her things. "Any luck?" I asked her.

"Not much. I was just going through Charles Fraser's diaries. I've looked through them before, but after Eliza's death, I figured they could use another look. How about you?"

I had completely forgotten what I'd even been doing downstairs before getting knocked out, but now it came crashing back to me.

"I had some luck," I said. "I think I found the place the letter was describing, St. Phillip's Church."

"St. Phillip's. It makes sense as a burial ground, but how did you come upon it?"

"It was once used as part of Charleston Harbor's navigational system. Holy light and savior of ships, just like the message says. Put that with so many prominent people being buried in its cemetery I figure it had to be our place."

"You might be right," Hannah said. "We'll check it out, but for now let's find you that ice."

Hannah put her bag across her should and then grabbed my hand in hers, leading out us of the reading room.

"And a drink," I said smiling at her.

"Fine, and a drink."

CHAPTER 27

In Charleston, the fog creeps in from the Atlantic Ocean, through the tight neck of the harbor entrance, and spreads like tendrils down the two rivers that border the peninsula city. As the fog grows thicker, and the waterways can no longer contain it, the streets gradually begin to fill. The fog escapes from the water and creeps steadily down the main avenues spreading and engulfing street lamps, buildings, and even the majestic oaks. Usually, just before the entire peninsula is swallowed up the sun will come to strength and battle back the intruder from the sea...usually.

Hannah had taken me home after the incident at the library. She had been an excellent nurse, getting me ice for my head and for my bourbon, all while making a fantastic dinner. When I woke the next morning, it was with a beautiful woman at my side and a renewed energy.

I slowly got out of bed, not to wake her, and went to the kitchen to start some coffee. With a fresh cup in hand, I went out on the porch to watch the fog slink its way down Church Street.

"Pretty spooky," Hannah said coming up behind me with a coffee mug in hand.

"Sure is, but beautiful in its own way."

"Seems odd that we are heading to a graveyard today and the fog rolls in."

"Are you scared?" I asked her with a smile.

"How's your head?" Hannah fired back ignoring my question.

I rubbed the back of my head still feeling the spot where I got hit. "A lot better. There's a little bump, but that's all."

"Good, then you should have no problem cooking me some breakfast."

"No problem at all." I smiled at her as I headed back inside to the kitchen.

We ate a simple breakfast of bacon, eggs over easy, and toast. Then got dressed and went to meet a colleague of Hannah's at the college. Professor Thompson specialized in Southern History and was a member and resident historian of St. Phillip's Church. We didn't want to go searching through a graveyard blind with no idea of what we were looking for. Hannah thought that Professor Thompson could possibly give us some insight.

The Professor chose not to meet us on campus, but instead opted for his home only a few blocks from where I was staying. Hannah and I poured ourselves a couple of cups of coffee for the road and walked from Church Street west down Tradd to Professor Thompson's residence. His home was a three-story Charleston Single with a double piazza and brick fence covered in creeping fig. We walked the drive along the side of the house and made our way to the rear, where the carriage house had been transformed into an office for the long-time teacher. Hannah gave a knock on the aged wooden door and almost immediately it began to creak open.

An older gentleman, tweed jacket, gingham shirt, pleated khakis and horned rimmed tortoise-shelled glasses answered our knock. His gray hair was balding and a little unkempt.

"Hannah," Professor Thompson said in a firm voice. "A pleasure to see you on this foggy morning."

"Glad you could see us, Professor. This is Jack Francis, who is working with me."

I found it odd Hannah addressed the man as professor, as I assumed they were equals. Maybe it was out of respect, so I followed suit. "Professor Thompson," I said shaking the man's hand, "nice to meet you."

"Nice to see you." He responded politely. "Refills on your coffee?"

"Yes, thank you," Hannah said.

The man topped off both of our mugs and then did the same to his own sitting on top of a large desk. He returned the pot and proceeded to take a seat, offering us a pair of worn leather chairs separated from his desk by an ornate rug. There was a fireplace at one end of the carriage house and a small kitchen at the other. A shaky staircase ascended to a loft on the second floor, and the walls on the first were covered with bookshelves and artifacts.

"What can I help you two with today?"

"I was wondering if you could tell us a little history about St. Phillip's Church and in particular its graveyard," Hannah asked.

"You two are busy people I assume, as am I, so you'll need to be more specific. The history of St. Phillip's is as old and long as the city itself."

"How about anything that stands out. What makes it unique or different from other churches in town?" I interjected.

"I see." The Professor said thinking. "I may have a few anecdotes that could be of interest to you."

CHAPTER 28

Unfortunately, Professor Thompson's history of St. Phillips was long, lectured, and leading us nowhere. I sat mostly staring into my empty coffee cup as he recounted the history of the congregation, the building of the first, second, and third church structures, and the history of some of its more famous members. If he were giving us a short history, I would have hated to hear the full version. I had almost entirely tuned out when Hannah finally interrupted the Professor with a question.

"They moved John Calhoun's body?" She asked.

"Why yes. Twice actually." The Professor answered.

"But why? Someone as respected as Calhoun, wouldn't it be sacrilegious to disturb his body?"

"Mr. Calhoun was revered in the city, the state, and throughout the South. Charleston was, as a whole, in a state of mourning when the Senator died. The town closed down, and everyone attended the funeral procession. In the present, John Calhoun is a representative of Southern beliefs even more than Southern politics, but in death, he became part of the Southern psyche."

"Then why move his body?" Hannah asked again.

"John Calhoun was a symbol of the South and the Confederacy. The citizens of Charleston worried that the approaching Union army would desecrate his remains, so they removed him from the western graveyard, and hid him near the temple in the east cemetery. After the war, he was returned to his original burial spot and in 1880 new construction began on the current monument in that location."

My mind began to move. The father of the Confederacy was too convenient, but the idea that he had been buried three times would give anyone a chance to hide something or change headstones. In my mind, the story led to a lot of possibilities.

"Was John Calhoun a Mason?" Hannah asked.

The professor looked at the Masonic ring on his finger and smiled. "No, Calhoun was not. I didn't take you as a conspiracy theorist."

"I'm not, but I also have to explore all avenues as a researcher. If only to rule them out."

"Very well." The Professor said.

The old man continued on with his lecture on the history of St. Phillip's, coming upon nothing more of our interest. When he was finished, Hannah and Professor Thompson exchanged a few tidbits of gossip at the college before we left.

"If that was a short and fascinating history of St. Phillip's I'd hate to have sat through the full version," I said to Hannah as we made our way down Tradd Street.

"He's a lecturer at heart and Southern. If he has an audience, he'll talk for days. We did get something from it, though."

"Yeah, that bit on Calhoun has got me curious. What was with your Mason question?"

"The hooked x on the letter. It still has me thrown."

"You thought if Calhoun were a Mason then we would have a clear answer?"

"One can hope, can't they?" Hannah gave a shrug of her shoulders as we walked. "I guess the next step is to head over to St. Phillip's and look things over for ourselves."

"Are you going to be okay with that?" I said looking at the fog still thick in the air. It was almost noon, and I was surprised the sun had not burned it off yet.

"I'll be fine." Hannah gave me a flirtatious punch in the shoulder. "And before you say anything I'm not afraid of the fog."

CHAPTER 29

When I was teasing Hannah about being afraid of the graveyard, I didn't realize how creepy it actually would be. St. Phillip's Church is in the center of downtown Charleston and only a few blocks from my Church Street carriage house, but the fog had wrapped itself tightly around each stone making it feel like you were all alone instead of in the middle of the city. You could hear the occasional sound of voices from within the fog as a group of tourist would pass by, and dark shadows could be seen walking in and out of the rows of headstones creating a ghostly effect.

Hannah and I made our way to the center of the western part of the cemetery across the street from the church building. Slowly, not to walk where we did not belong, Hannah led me to the center of the yard. A large rectangular object began to grow as we moved closer. It stood at least a foot over my head and was wider than my arms could stretch. It wasn't until I was nearly a foot from its base that I could read John Caldwell Calhoun carved across the side framed with a pair of columns in each corner of the monument. I had noticed the marker before when I had walked past the graveyard under more normal circumstances. It towered over the other markers in the western portion of the cemetery, and in a town with a history of significant people, Calhoun's headstone showed a distinctive recognition.

"This is the original and final resting spot of John Calhoun," Hannah said. "The stone memorial was added in 1880 as the Professor said."

"Any idea what we're looking for?"

"None and it will be hard to find anything in this fog. Let's work our way slowly around the burial site. Look for anything odd or out of the ordinary on the marker. If you see something on one side that's not on the other, or anything along those lines let me know. After that, we will slowly make our way out. There may be another marker buried within the site."

"I'll do my best," I said back to her, as a dark shape past us in the fog and then a second later a camera flash went off. *What could anyone be photographing in this fog*, I thought.

Hannah and I made our way around the stone memorial a couple times, going over its detailed carvings from top to bottom and back again. Nothing stood out. I found nothing, no hooked x, no mysterious riddles or numbers, nothing but a prestigious monument to a former Vice-President.

"Let's start checking the grass," Hannah said.

We squatted low and made circles, beginning close to the monument and working our way out. It was painful looking, moving, and squatting all at the same time and I was a little happy when I finally began edging closer to the black shape in the fog. I had assumed it was a stone from the nearby burial site, and I was right, but I wasn't prepared for the skull that suddenly came clear through the fog. It gave me a spook, and I jumped out of my crouched position.

"What is it?"

"Nothing," I said to Hannah. "I just came upon the next grave a little faster than I thought in this fog."

Hannah walked closer to me and smiled when she saw the skull on the headstone. "That's death's head," Hannah said. "Early headstone carving in the Colonies avoided using religious figures, so death's head was cut onto the stones to represent the physical and spiritual death of the individual. Basically, it means that it's an old tombstone, so be careful."

"Spooky," I muttered under my breath. "I didn't find anything, so what now?"

"Let's head over to the eastern portion where Calhoun's body was hidden from Union troops. His family is also buried over on that side, so we'll examine their plot too."

"His family. Why aren't they buried together?" I asked.

"No matter how respected John Calhoun was in South Carolina he could never be buried in the eastern portion of the cemetery because you must be born in Charleston to be interned there. His wife was a Charlestonian and his children were born in the city, so the family's final resting place is there while John's is here across the street."

"Every day I'm in Charleston I learn of new and often strange customs. For a city that thrives on tourism, many of their rituals aren't exactly inviting to outsiders."

"Charlestonians make great hosts and hostesses, but you will never become accepted as one, no matter how long you're here. Charleston isn't like other cities where money often buys acceptance. Here you need money and lineage."

CHAPTER 30

The eastern graveyard was more crowded with headstones and tourists. It was a spot where Charleston's most well-known residents were buried, from Confederate heroes to signers of the Declaration of Independence and the Constitution. There were more dark shadows, voices in the fog, and flashes going off. *Why were they taking pictures in a graveyard full of fog?* Many of the stones were beautifully carved, but I couldn't see so how could the camera?

"In the north corner, behind the church, there is a temple building, and Calhoun's body was placed there during the war years," Hannah said motioning me along.

Massive columns began to rise from the ground as we wound our way around gravestones and along a skinny path. A gothic structure that mimicked the larger church began to become visible through the fog and towering live oaks. Gravestones had been cemented into the walls along the outer side of the building, with others simply leaning against one and other. Hannah moved slowly around the temple building and made her way to its southern face. The outer wall was covered with grave markers cemented into its side as she motioned me under an expansive oak tree.

"What is with all the markers along the cemetery walls and here on the temple?" I asked Hannah.

"When a headstone is removed from its original location it is no longer a marker for a grave, but instead a memorial. Many of these represent burial sites that have disappeared over time or as memorials to loved ones. This one here is not only a memorial but also a marker to where someone was once buried."

I looked up to see a plaque on the temple wall that read Calhoun in big bold letters, with a paragraph of smaller text scribed into the bottom of the stone.

"That marble slab once covered Calhoun's tomb for 34 years in the western cemetery before he was buried here during the war," Hannah said.

I moved closer to get a better look, leaving Hannah to stand by the old oak tree. Bending down I got a closer look at the paragraph carved into the bottom of the stone.

"My brethren, be not many masters, knowing that we shall receive the greater condemnation. For in many things, we offend all. If any man offend not in word, the same is a perfect man, and able also to bridle the whole body. Behold, we put bits in the horses' mouths, that they may obey us; and we turn about their whole body. Behold also the ships, which though they be so great, and are driven of fierce winds, yet are they turned about with a very small helm, whithersoever the governor listeth. Even so, the tongue is a little member, and boasteth great things. Behold, how great a matter a little fire kindleth! And the tongue is a fire, a world of iniquity: so is the tongue among our members, that it defileth the whole body, and setteth on fire the course of nature; and it is set on fire of hell." I read the paragraph out loud.

"I'm not sure what the whole thing means," Hannah said, "but I can grasp that it is along the lines of the power of the spoken word. An interesting choice, considering Calhoun's fame as an orator."

I turned from the marker and began to walk back towards Hannah when I noticed old markings carved into the tree behind her.

"Look at this," I said moving past her. On the tree, I could barely make out the letter J.A.M. roughly carved and scared into the bark. "It's the same as in the letter."

Hannah moved closer in for a look and then made her way around the rest of the large trunk. "Jack look at this. The hooked x."

On the opposite side of the tree, and scared into the trunk, was a roughly carved hooked x, small and barely visible to the casual observer.

"What does it mean?" I asked.

"I'm not sure, but we are definitely on to something."

I spotted another shadow in the fog moving past us, and suddenly another camera flashed.

"We need to go," I whispered.

"You might be right," Hannah said leading the way towards the front of the graveyard and back onto Church Street.

CHAPTER 31

"The letter, do you have it?" George Trenholm boomed at me from across the desk in his study.

I was getting tired of being summoned to his house like one of his servants. "Why would you think that I have it?" I said calmly.

"You and that northern professor have been snooping around some pretty odd places. What does the Historical Society and St. Phillip's Church have to do with my son's murder?" Trenholm threw some photos of us in the graveyard on his desk.

"Why don't you tell me?" I was totally ignoring the fact that he was obviously having me followed for the moment.

"How should I know?"

"Then why would you believe we have your letter, simply by the places Hannah and I have been visiting? There has been a lot you haven't told me. Why? I'm not sure. Maybe it's because you don't believe it has anything to do with Jason's murder, or maybe it's because family secrets are more valuable to keep than finding your son's killer."

Trenholm sat in his leather desk chair, chin to his chest, looking down at his lap and exposing too much of his neck fat. Silent, and like a rock, his stubbornness told me a lot about the main and the beliefs he held.

"What's so remarkable about that letter? Someone broke in here looking for it, and now you assume I have it. Why does an old piece of paper seem to be the main key to your son's death, and yet you refuse to help me understand."

"Who says you didn't have someone break into my study just to get your hands on it?" Trenholm finally spoke.

"Don't be so daft. You're a smart man, but now your stubbornness is making you ignorant."

"Oh, I don't believe the man who broke in has any connection to you. I actually believe that professor got the letter from Jason. I know they were working together on a little family history...not sure how he found it, though."

"Once again you're missing the point. I need to know why that letter is so important if I'm going to help find your son's killer."

"Your job is to protect this family by conducting your own investigation into Jason's murder." Trenholm stood with hands on his desk, voice reaching a stern tone. "All you appear to be doing is uncovering town gossip. I believe I'm done with your services. And I want you to give that letter back to me."

"Fine, but I don't have the letter." I smiled calmly back at him.

"I'll have the authorities after you and that woman for theft."

"I don't think so. You don't want anyone else knowing about that old piece of paper." I got up from my seat and headed towards the door. "If I come across it though I'll let you know. Oh, and you can send my final check over to Mrs. Legare's carriage house." With one last smile at the red-faced man, I left.

CHAPTER 32

I knew there wasn't going to be another check forthcoming from Mr. Trenholm, but it was a satisfying final jab to irritate the man. I had no intention of stopping my investigation, partly for my own curiosities and partly to help my nephew Bryce find some answers. I detested people like George Trenholm. The man felt he was special because of his birthright and, unfortunately, this perception was only reinforced by most citizens in Charleston. That's not how I was raised, and I saw each man for the man he was, not for the man his ancestors were, and Trenholm was a rich asshole. It was that simple. How could someone care more about the family's reputation then finding his son's killer?

Part of me realized that I wanted to continue the investigation for selfish reasons. I wanted to know what Trenholm was hiding and put the man in a place he deserved. If that was possible. I know that the rich usually find a way to wiggle out of responsibility, and often someone below them takes the brunt of their actions, but I had to try to expose whatever family secret Trenholm was so desperate to hide. I wondered if it would even be shocking enough to penetrate the fortress that was Charleston's high society, but I was going to find out one way or another.

"I got fired," I said to Hannah, as I came up the stairs of the carriage house.

"Oh, you poor baby." The woman was holding a glass of wine in her hand and sarcasm in her voice.

"I'll take one of those," pointing to her drink.

Hannah poured me a heavy glass from the bottle of Washington State pinot noir she had on the counter. "Here you go. Now go take a hot shower. I'll have dinner ready by the time you get out."

"Dinner? Are we playing house already?"

"Don't worry Mr. Francis I'm not looking for a husband, I'm just hungry. Now, go take a shower. We have a lot to go over. Unless, you're not moving forward since you've been fired."

"Oh, I'm definitely moving forward…especially since I got fired, even if it's just to piss on Trenholm's happy life a little bit."

I went to the bedroom and got undressed before grabbing my robe and heading to the shower. I realized underneath the hot water that I had not smelled any food coming from the kitchen, and it was only after the water was shut off that I heard voices. *Take-out*, I thought with a smile, as I was drying off.

A pair of jeans hung over the back of the chair in my bedroom, and I quickly threw a Chief Wahoo t-shirt on with them. I pulled a pair of boat shoes from the closet and made my way back to Hannah and our take-out dinner.

She was standing perfectly still, leaning on the kitchen counter with her wine still in hand. Something in the living area had her eye, and she didn't break her glance to look at me as I made my way towards her. It wasn't until I was standing nearly next to her that I realized a man was standing in the room holding a brilliantly shined sword, dressed as a tour guide, and brandishing a wicked smile.

"Mr. Francis, how nice of you to join us. I take it you enjoyed your shower." The man said in a thick southern drawl that resembled the Upcountry more than the Charleston tongue I was getting used to.

"What are you doing here?" I asked surprisingly calm.

"I'm here to talk, as long as the two of you don't do anything stupid."

"About what?"

"Confederate treasure, Mr. Francis."

CHAPTER 33

The man before me was a bit disheveled and unkempt. His hair was long and stringy, tucked back and underneath a Confederate cap. He wore a white shirt marked with dirt stains and infantry gray pants with a scuffed and worn pair of boots. The only thing about him that was perfect was the blade in his hand.

The intruder smiled at me before he spoke again, revealing the yellow teeth of a smoker or coffee drinker. "I believe the two of you have something I've been searching for." He said.

"I'm not sure what you mean, and who the hell are you?" I asked a little less calm than before.

"Elliott Tidwell, a descendant of Edward Tidwell, loyal servant of the Confederacy. Now that we know each other...where is that letter?"

"Locked up in my office?" Hannah finally spoke.

"I've already searched there. You are lying?"

"No, I'm not. I figured since my office had already been broken into that it was now a safe place."

Hannah had the letter on her, she always did, but her tactics were sound.

"What's your need for that letter?" I asked Tidwell.

"Oh, nothing more than restoring my family's name and ruining the family that ruined mine."

"Revenge is a powerful motivator, but it still doesn't answer what part that letter plays."

Tidwell sneered at me for a moment. "The letter is the key that leads to the lost Confederate treasure, and it's proof that the Trenholm's stole it from its rightful owners."

"Who are the rightful owners? Wouldn't the gold belong to the Federal Government now?"

The sneer on Tidwell's face grew at the mention of the US Government. "That treasure belongs to the Knights of the Golden Circle, who were charged to protect it for the Southern people until the time when they could once again break free of the iron grip this country has on them."

I saw a light turn on somewhere inside of Hannah, but I was just as clueless as before. "The Knights of the Golden Circle?"

"Are none of your business, Yankee." The man nearly screamed at me.

"How did the Trenholm's bring ruin to your family?" Hannah spoke up.

"George Trenholm was Secretary of the Treasury for the Confederacy. When Richmond was evacuated, he was charged with bringing the Confederate gold out of Richmond and to South

Carolina, where it could be transported to safety in England. Trenholm marched south with President Davis and then broke off when they reached the South Carolina backcountry. Half of the treasure was to be loaded onto blockade runners somewhere south of Charleston and the other half north of the city. Edward Tidwell was put in charge of the delivering the half of the treasure that was heading north of the city. The plan was for him and a group of his men to meet up with Trenholm's party near Elliott, South Carolina, where they would split the gold. Trenholm would take half and continue South towards Charleston, and my ancestor would take his half to a location along the Santee. When they arrived at Eldorado Plantation and prepared to load the gold onto flatboats, it was discovered that the treasure had been replaced with brick covered in straw."

"Wait, they took the gold to a place called Eldorado Plantation. Was that on purpose." I had to ask.

"Shut up you fool. The plantation had already been attacked by a Union gunboat on the river, and like your professor friend it was thought that since the Union troops had already been there they would not be returning anytime soon."

"What happened to all the gold then?" I asked.

"Edward Tidwell and his men were accused of stealing it, loading bricks in its stead in hopes that nothing would be revealed until the ship made its way to England. They were relieved of their duties, banished from the KGC, and my family name became synonymous with treason in the South. But Edward Tidwell was played the fool by Trenholm and my family has suffered for that man's greed."

"Why do you believe Trenholm stole the treasure?" Hannah asked.

"Because he was the only other person with access. My family did not take that gold. Our miserable life since the war should bear witness to our innocence, while the Trenholms have grown more affluent and prosperous."

"But they were already wealthy."

"That may be true, but Fraser, Trenholm, and Company were going to take a massive financial hit from the debts owed to it from the Confederacy, which would never be paid, and from the Union for treason. The gold in the Confederate Treasury would not only keep them afloat but allow them to grow."

It made sense, and it wasn't the first time the scenario had been up for discussion. "Why do you want the letter then? Wouldn't the treasure be long gone and spent by now?" I asked knowing our time for talk was running short.

"The map will lead to where the treasure was hidden whether there is anything left or not is none of my concern. The gold belonged to the Southern people, not my family. The map is a connection to prove that the Trenholms took the gold and hid it after the war. The letter will lead me to the spot, and that spot will be somewhere with a strong connection to George Trenholm."

"You know that for sure?"

"Enough of your questions." The man moved closer to Hannah and me with his sword. "I want the letter."

"All right," Hannah said, "enough talk. My keys are in my purse. I'll need them to get into my office." She pointed to her purse sitting on a desk behind Tidwell.

The man had a decision to make. He couldn't keep us both covered with only a sword if he had to turn to grab the keys or allow Hannah to get them. He would have to make a decision, and when Tidwell made his choice, I would make my move.

CHAPTER 34

Hannah took a step towards her purse, moving slowly at first. Tidwell didn't budge and appeared to be allowing her to grab her keys. Right before she reached the desk, Tidwell reached out, grabbed Hannah by the arm, and pulled her close to him. With one arm around her chest and the other holding the sword blade up to her neck, the man smiled at me. His yellowed teeth glared at me, and I wanted to punch them out.

"Don't move an inch, Mr. Francis." He slowly backed up towards the desk while still facing me. He glanced back slightly when he came within inches of the wooden antique. "Now, reach for your purse." He said to Hannah, moving just enough for her to reach back and grab it.

"Take the purse and leave. There is no need to get violent." I said to Tidwell.

"No, there isn't, unless you do something stupid. Why would I let her go? All you two would do is call the police and have them waiting for me at her office."

Tidwell inched closer with Hannah towards the door and the stairwell that led down to the driveway. I knew it would be tricky for him to navigate the stairs with Hannah, and I hoped to have the opportunity to disrupt the situation.

With a sneer still on his face, Tidwell sidestepped closer and closer to the door. Finally, using the hand holding Hannah by the chest he reached behind him and opened the door to the stairwell. It took him a couple tries to blindly find the door knob before he was able to grab hold and swing the door open, leaving an open stairwell behind him.

Suddenly, before he could return his arm to its position around Hannah's chest, she brought her foot up and slammed it down hard against the man's shin. Tidwell lit out a yell and loosened the sword's position from Hannah's neck. Hannah dropped to her knees, as I charged forward. The pain in his leg and seeing me attacking caused a limped Tidwell to flinch. He lost his balance and struggled to regain it before his momentum finally propelled him down the stairs behind him.

The sound of him falling, body on wood and the steel sword blade on the plaster walls made a loud racket that echoed back up the stairs. When it was over, Tidwell laid at the bottom motionless on the brick pathway.

I waited for a second, gave Hannah a looked that asked if she was all right, and then started slowly down the steps towards the man. I made it to the last few steps when the man jumped up with a yell, brandishing the sword and swinging it in front of my face. As unexpectedly as he started, he stopped. Tidwell only stared at me, burning rage building in his eyes and teeth grinding with hate. I prepared for him to attack, waiting for the sword to come at me again, but instead he turned and ran down the driveway into the darkness of the night.

Standing there motionless, I watched the spot in the darkness where the strange man had disappeared, expecting him to return. I felt Hannah approach from behind me, putting her arms around my waist and her chin on my shoulder.

"Are you all right?" I asked.

"I'm fine, heartbeat is finally settling down. Now come on back upstairs…fear turns me on." Out of the corner of my eye I could see a smile, and I knew she wasn't kidding.

CHAPTER 35

I woke up the next morning with Hannah next to me on her laptop drinking coffee. I could see her purse on the table next to the bed and had a quick flashback of the night before.

"You're up early."

"You slept late. There's fresh coffee if you want some." She said not looking away from the computer screen.

"What are you doing?"

Hannah ignored me for a second as she concentrated, reading something intently. "There is a professor I work with at Columbia. An older gentleman, who doesn't teach much anymore."

"Emeritus status?" I asked.

"Something like that. Anyways, he did a study on the Knights of the Golden Circle or the KGC back in the seventies. I'm looking for his paper in the university files."

"I'll let you get to it," I said getting out of bed and heading for the coffee.

After a few minutes on the porch and a wave to Mrs. Legare working on her flowers, I returned to the bedroom with my coffee to find Hannah getting off of her cell phone.

"My office was broken into last night again." She said.

"I'm not surprised."

"Neither am I, but the school's starting to get a little upset about it. They don't like the added attention, especially because it's from a visiting professor."

"Any luck finding that paper?"

"Yeah, I found it right before the phone rang."

Hannah went right back to reading as I settled into bed and turned the flat screen on to ESPN. Baseball season was in its infancy, and I was excited about the prospects for my Indians. We sat there without a word for almost forty-five minutes and two cups of coffee before Hannah spoke again.

"Well, that explains the hooked x and the carving on the tree." She said.

"Do you mind explaining it all to me?"

"It appears that the KGC was founded in either Cincinnati or Lexington Kentucky around 1854 by General George Bickley. The idea behind the organization, with the support of a lot of Northern sympathizers, was to create a nation from the Southern States, Mexico, Latin America, and the

Caribbean with Havana at its center. The idea was to form a golden circle around these territories, reinforce their slave status, and create a monopoly on the sugar, cotton, and tobacco producing regions. However, these initial plans were aborted around 1860 to focus on the coming civil war in the States." Hannah began.

She started skimming her computer again, and I waited patiently for several minutes.

"There is a lot of myth surrounding the group, and separating fact from fiction seems to be impossible." She started up again. "But it appears that the society gained popularity and support during the war, both in the North and the South. The military wing of the organization is said to be the foundation of the Ku Klux Klan, and there is even mention of Jesse James and John Wilkes Booth being members."

"That would explain the date on the letter."

"Maybe. Where it really gets interesting and relevant to us is after the war. Apparently, the organization was collecting mass quantities of wealth to support a future war for independence and established an intricate system of codes to hide their treasures. Even more relevant is the connection of prominent Southern Masons to the organization, which would explain the hooked x. If the KGC borrowed from their Mason brethren, it would make sense, and the J.A.M. on the letter and on the tree at St. Phillip's would have to be some sort of code used to designate an area or where the next clue lies."

"I've got questions."

"I'm sure you do," Hannah said with a smile, finally looking up from her laptop.

"First, how do we decipher the codes?"

"Professor Avery, in his work, describes how the ciphers functioned in some detail."

"Okay, then my next question is…if George Trenholm stole the Confederate gold, why did he use KGC codes to hide it?"

Hannah looked perplexed for a moment. "I don't have an answer for that. Maybe he was a member, and it was a system he was familiar with. Maybe it's a similar system with personal changes or possibly we are way off our mark."

"One last question and it's bothered me since last night. If Edward Tidwell was supposed to take half of the Confederate Treasury with him north of Charleston, what happened to the other half that George Trenholm was transferring south of the city?"

"Now that is something I hadn't thought of," Hannah said.

CHAPTER 36

Hannah had left to teach a class and see how bad of a mess her office was in. I had showered and moved to the porch with my laptop, studying up on what I did not know about the KGC. I was watching a carriage pass and listening to the tour guide tell an exaggerated truth about the house across the street when my phone rang.

"Colin," I answered, "how's Cleveland?"

"Cloudy, cold, and rainy…beautiful as always." His scruffy voice responded. "I've got something you might be interested in."

"What's that?"

"You were interested in a bookie by the name of Tommy Makem?"

"Yeah," I answered, having nearly forgotten about the man with everything else going on. "Did you find something new?"

"Could be nothing, could be something, but I figured I would pass it along. I asked around, and it seems that Tommy got into some trouble as a young man. He was working for a local bookie from a westside neighborhood, learning the business when he beat a man to death. Apparently, the man owed money and Tommy was determined to beat it out of him. Word is that he didn't mean to kill him, but Tommy got carried away with his work."

"Do I need to ask why there wasn't an arrest file?"

"There was never an arrest because there were no witnesses. The man's death was blamed on a mugging gone badly, and the rest is just neighborhood gossip."

"Shocking," I said sarcastically.

"After, Tommy left Cleveland, spent some time in Chicago with an uncle who paid for him to go to college, and finally chose to settle in Charleston for no apparent reason."

"So Tommy's a college educated bookie with street smarts…that's a wicked combination."

"And a possible history of violence," Colin said.

"I'm not really surprised." Men like Tommy usually had a history of violence, it came with the territory. "Thanks for the info Colin. How's Katya doing?"

"She's good. Been busy getting the restaurant ready for Indians' season. Looks like we may have a team this year and the whole town is buzzing with excitement."

"I've been trying to keep up, but it's not the same as being there. There is nothing better than walking into a bar and the whole room is talking about one team. Down here there are no loyalties. The locals don't have a team, and everyone else comes from somewhere else…no sense of community support like there is back home."

"Getting homesick?" Colin asked.

"A little. Maybe I'll come back when the weather warms up for good."

"We'll be here waiting for you. Let me know if I can be of any more help to you."

"Thanks, Colin. Tell Katya I said hi." I hung up the phone and thought about our conversation for a moment.

I had only been gone from Cleveland a couple months, but there was something about the start of a new baseball season that could always make you a little homesick. I also pondered what Colin had said about Tommy Makem. Neighborhood gossip was often stronger than any police report. It could have been a simple act of his youth, or the beginning of a pattern. Jason's murder did resemble the incident that Colin had described Tommy being involved in back in his Cleveland days. Eliza Dunn's death was better orchestrated and involved planning, Jason's didn't have that same appearance. Maybe our first impressions were right, and there was only one killer, but maybe we were wrong, and now two killers were running around Charleston.

CHAPTER 37

My review of the history of the KGC found them to be a highly organized and complex society. The KGC was furnished with an elaborate military division, extensive ritual, and a system of governance similar to the Masons. Eligibility for membership included all Southerners of good character and worthy Northern men who were determined to stand by the Constitutional rights of the South. The society was divided into three distinct degrees with the first being entirely military and chivalry based. The Second Degree was established to pursue the commercial and financial aspects of the society, which were charged with supply, support, and propaganda. The Third Degree and the highest to achieve, called the American Legion, was the political and governing arm of the KGC. Membership in the Third Degree appeared to be extremely secretive with members not being known to the lesser degrees.

With organizations like the KGC, soldiers, or those of the lowest degree, often did not know who was giving orders or why. It allowed for the society to contain its deepest secrets, its master plan, or its real purpose to be hidden from the view of outsiders. As I read, I wondered if it wasn't possible that Edward Tidwell and his men had been mere soldiers in the KGC and used by a member of the Third Degree, such as George Trenholm. Was it possible that the plan all along for the KGC was to set up Tidwell and his men to further throw others off the trail? The more I read the more I was beginning to realize the story may have a lot more twists than Hannah and I first realized.

On top of the organizational structure of the KGC, their secret codes used to locate treasures caches, seemed to be surrounded by the most mystery. A combination of Masonic symbols, religious references, and part pirate treasure map it seemed the KGC code could involve a lot of interpretation. It would allow someone like George A. Trenholm to use the system in his own way if he did indeed steal the Confederate gold for himself while, on the other side, it was plausible that Trenholm was a member of the KGC and the codes we came across were authorized through the society. I certainly hoped Hannah was reading up too, and I had to have faith she could interpret all of this better than I could.

Hannah, I knew, would be on top of the research, it was in her nature, but I had to check in on Tommy Makem. Colin's phone call reminded me that I had another lead that I had forgotten to follow up, and I figured it was time to join the bookie for another chit-chat over happy hour. The Tidwells, KGC, and millions in Confederate gold would have to wait. Makem seemed like the least likely suspect, but a suspect none-the-less, so I needed to dig a little deeper. The man appeared to be a talker, a typical characteristic for someone as confident as Makem, so maybe a friendly conversation would reveal something I had missed before.

CHAPTER 38

"Well, Mr. Jack Francis, how's my favorite Ohioan in Charleston?"

"Not too bad Tommy," I said to Makem as I came up the stairs of the Cocktail Club.

"Are you here to see me? I have to assume you are since you don't frequent this establishment all that often."

"If you don't, mind I would like to run a few things by you."

"Why not? Although I'm not sure why you're still going around asking questions into Jason Trenholm's murder. Word on the street is that the old man fired you." Makem said with a smile as he offered the bar stool next to him.

"Call it professional curiosity."

Makem waved the bartender down our way and ordered a pair of bourbons, Blanton's this time with two cubes a piece. He waited for the bartender to bring the drinks, thanking her when she placed them in front of the two of us.

"Now," he began, "what can I do for you today?"

"I got a phone call from an old friend backup in Cleveland. He had an interesting story about a young Tommy Makem. Apparently, it's rumored that you took a man's life over a debt owed back in the day."

"I do miss the old neighborhood. I'm not sure what incident you're talking about, but I was just an apprentice back in my Cleveland days. I didn't have the authority to go after someone like that."

He didn't deny or admit to anything, just skipped around the truth. "Why did you leave Cleveland then?"

"I had an uncle in Chicago who thought I was going down a dangerous path. My father was never around, and my mother was overwhelmed with such a large family. He took me off her hands, raised me and sent me off to college."

"So it had nothing to do with the reports of you beating a man to death?"

Makem smiled at me and took a sip of his drink. "Not that I'm aware of. My mother and my uncle had been planning it for months. She knew it would be the only way I would ever get to go to school and get out of Cleveland."

I took my drink, gave it a swirl, and thought for a moment. Even though Makem was skimming the boundaries between truth and fiction, I knew that he was still telling me a lot. I had to listen to him and find somewhere between his words what it was that he was really telling me.

"Where did you end up going to school?" I asked him.

"The Citadel. My uncle thought it best that I went somewhere that I wouldn't have a lot of room to get in trouble." Makem twisted the giant Citadel ring on his hand. "It is how I came to fall in love with Charleston."

The Citadel was the military college of South Carolina, nestled in the northern part of the peninsula between the Ashley River and Hampton Park. The school was known for providing an excellent education while developing talented young soldiers. The education Makem had received there would have paired well with the education he got growing up in Cleveland's poor Irish neighborhoods. An excellent balance between a street thug polished soldier, and genteel scholar. It also made me think that he might be above a simple beat-down for an unpaid debt, maybe.

"Did you stay here after graduation?" I asked Makem.

"Oh no, I moved around, traveled, and saw the world before I decided to come back here and settle down."

"I'm sure being a former Cadet helped you get intertwined in Charleston society."

"If you're asking if it helped me find customers like Jason Trenholm then the answer is yes. In Charleston, it is all about who you know."

"I'm beginning to learn that," I said finishing off my drink.

"Can I get you another one?" Makem asked pointing to my glass.

"No thank you, and this rounds on me." I stood up and threw some cash on the bar. "One's enough for me, but thanks for the talk."

"Never a problem. You know where to find me if you want to do it again." Makem said with a grin.

"You never know I just might."

CHAPTER 39

It wasn't until late the following afternoon that I saw Hannah again. When I heard someone coming up the stairs, I expected her to be weighed down with books and information from researching the KGC further. Instead, she held a tablet in a black leather case. I suddenly became aware that the days of poring over old manuscripts in libraries were slowly coming to an end.

"You look tired," I said to her.

"Thanks a lot. I was up most of the night reading and taking notes. It appears that the KGC was a complicated bunch."

"I was starting to get that impression through my reading as well." I thought about updating her on Colin's phone call and Tommy Makem but decided to wait. She looked like she was about to get on a roll.

"I did a little background study, and there wasn't much proven about the KGC, a whole lot of conspiracy and maybes but no hard evidence. That said, they did exist, and there does seem to be a code. I went into the database at Columbia and found some notes and information about their systems and how to translate them. Once again, no hard evidence and no guarantees. The codes system seems to involve a lot of interpretation. All my notes are on here." She said holding up the tablet. "I figure we go back to St. Phillip's and begin there."

"Sounds good to me. Besides, I've got a few things to update you on while we walk there."

We made our way the few blocks north to St. Phillip's and I filled her in on Makem. She didn't seem too intrigued by the whole exchange until I mentioned that Makem was a Citadel alum, then her eyes gave way to a brief flicker. It disappeared almost immediately as we entered the cemetery and I forgot about it as quickly as Hannah did.

"Okay," she said pulling out the tablet, "There are a few core elements to the KGC code that we need to be aware of. First, the KGC were masters of misdirection who intentionally loaded their carvings with false leads. They were betting that most treasure hunters would get so exasperated after chasing these false clues, they'd give up before they ever found anything. We need to look for a couple things carved into trees, rocks or even headstones. Animals are travel symbols that when combined with other clues can represent direction and distance. Carvings of ghosts will tell us that the next clue is located on a grave. A heart or the letter H stands for the middle. Any numerals can either tell you how far to go or might send you to a nearby object with that many sides."

Hannah paused for a moment to make sure I was retaining everything she had said. Scrolling through the tablet, she began again.

"As you can tell, this isn't a simple process. There are hundreds of such symbols, which can produce a near-infinite number of combinations, and are up for interpretations. When you are looking at gravestones, look for misspellings, another clue. Finally, and above all, the KGC code seems to rely heavily upon biblical chapter and verse. I assume because all of its members would've known it well, as good Southern Christians." Hannah exclaimed with a slight smile. "A cryptic carving might direct you to a verse in the Bible, or be a verse from the Bible, and then the interpretation of that would further guide you to another symbol."

I had to admit it was a lot to take on and my brain was already numb.

"I guess we'll start at Calhoun's grave then?"

"Not his grave," Hannah said. "His false grave."

CHAPTER 40

It had been foggy the last time we set foot in St. Phillip's Cemetery. Now, the skies were clear, the sun shining, and squirrels jumped between branches on the ancient oak trees. There was one tree in particular that had our eye, and today I could see it more clearly than I did the last time I stood underneath it.

Whether it was because of the fog or because I hadn't known at the time what to look for, I hadn't realized that the tree across from the spot where Calhoun was buried during the Civil War was covered with carved objects. Previously, the hooked x and *J.A.M.* were the only two carvings that caught my eye, but now there were hundreds of symbols, animals, numbers, and faces etched into the trunk.

"How did we miss all this?" I said to Hannah. "And what does it all mean?"

"I have to assume that most of it means nothing, and simply are here to provide cover for the actual clues."

Hannah began taking pictures with her tablet. She shot the tree trunk from a multitude of angles. Then Hannah took a three-hundred-and-sixty-degree view of the cemetery from the base of the tree. Finally, she focused in on Calhoun's memorial stone back on the wall of the temple building. I watched as she snapped a photo, highlighted the scribed writing at the bottom of the monument, and began a search. In second she had an assortment of option explain the location of the stone, the history of Calhoun's resting spots, and finally something new.

"We should have known. Scripture. James 3." Hannah said of the words at the bottom of Calhoun's memorial stone.

"James 3," I said out loud as I thought about the letter, the tree, and the two of us now standing in the cemetery hunting for buried treasure. "James 3…I've got it. The letter and the tree are both marked with *J.A.M.*, which call me crazy, but I think stands for James 3. You said the KGC used scripture so this fits. The letter J, A, and M could stand for James and the three dots could represent the third book."

"I have to admit it makes sense, but what is the clue telling us?"

"I'm not sure we have it all. Either we are missing something on the memorial stone, or we are missing something on the tree. Both the letter and the tree have a hooked x, maybe that is something."

"Possibly, but it may just be used to help mark the trail." Hannah started going through the pictures she took of the tree trunk, changing the filter, so the carvings stood out more. "I've counted three-ghost carvings on the tree all exactly alike. There are a dozen animals, but each one is different. Five human faces all different, and numbers ranging from zero to thirty-three with none repeating."

"The ghosts, are they exactly the same?" As Hannah double checked her pictures, I went to the tree to examine it more carefully.

"Yes, exactly alike."

"I agree," I said finding them on the tree trunk. "You said ghosts represent a clue pointing towards a gravestone, so we are going to look for a headstone."

"But why three ghosts?"

"Maybe we are looking for three headstones. Let's start with the tree as the center and slowly make circles outward."

We began slowly on separate sides of the tree tracing over each other's steps as we worked outward. Graveyards as old as the one at St. Phillip's Church were hard to negotiate. For every stone that had been meticulously taken care of there was one that had been neglected and crumbled. Others had been worn by the weather of the years, and their effigies were no longer visible. Slowly we walked. Slowly, hunched over we read every marker we passed.

"Jack, I've got something."

CHAPTER 41

Flush with the ground and half buried in leaves was a rectangular stone with the word JAMES carved into it. Behind stood three headstones of different ages, beginning with A. JAMES and ending with A. JAMES III.

"The James Family plot and just our luck there was an A. James the third," I said to Hannah after I made my way over to her.

"Three generations of Charlestonians, Southerners, and merchants."

"How do you figure?" I asked.

"Along the top of each gravestone is carved a rope outlining a ship. The thickness of the line indicates the wealth of the family, and the James' had a thick rope."

I gave a small giggle.

"What?"

"Nothing, except usually if you feel the need to show the world how thick your rope is..."

"Don't finish that thought." Hannah interrupted. "Look each headstone has a name, date, and an inscription."

Hannah took pictures with her tablet once again and did searches of each headstone.

"Odd." She said, almost to herself.

"What is it?"

"The inscription on the grandfather and father are both from the Bible, but the son's inscription doesn't appear to be."

"Only through the four points of God's cross can heaven be found." I read out loud. "Sounds like scripture to me."

"But it's not." Hannah was quiet for a moment. "It's a clue, but to what exactly I don't know."

"Jason gives you a letter he finds in his father's study with invisible ink *J.A.M.* is inscribed on it. We are guided to this cemetery where we find the same carved into a tree and a memorial to the spot where John C. Calhoun was once buried marked with a passage from the book of James. Now I'm staring at the grave marker of A. James III. There is an obvious common theme here."

"Yes, but where does it lead? Also, the KGC were cryptic at best and insane at worst when leaving clues. The theme at this clue may be just that, and when we move forward, it could change. Also, something as obvious as the James' name could be a cold trail offered to mislead treasure hunters." Hannah seemed frustrated.

We stood in silence as she furiously tapped at the screen of her tablet, swiping up and down looking at pages as fast as she could.

"Worthless." She said after about five minutes.

"What's worthless?"

"The damn internet. There is nothing on the James Family here in Charleston. And from their burial plot the family either died out or moved after A. James III was buried."

I looked around, and even though there was room, there were no more headstones dedicated to the James' name.

"I need to do it the old fashioned way and head to the library. Apparently, there is still a need for those houses of knowledge and wisdom." Hannah began to walk towards the street.

"Do you want to look around a bit more, maybe we missed something."

"We probably did, but I can't focus until I have answers. Besides, I took pictures of everything for reference."

You could see her frustration, but also understand her dedication to research. Hannah was the type of woman who fed off of knowledge, and when a question arose that she couldn't answer she had to find it immediately. The longer she went without finding it only frustrated her more. I respected that, knew it fueled an ambitious woman.

CHAPTER 42

I went with Hannah over to the Historical Society library for a little while, but Bryce and Sarah had wanted to see me for a late lunch. The two newlyweds were finally leaving on their delayed honeymoon and wanted to say goodbye. I hoped, and as I'm sure did they, that my business in Charleston would be resolved by the time they returned. We dined at SNOB once again and avoided speaking of Jason's death, the investigation, or the fact that Mr. Trenholm fired me. I'm sure they both knew about it and only were trying to avoid any depressing or awkward conversation during our last lunch together.

After lunch and a few heartfelt goodbyes, I decided to walk home and try to relax for the rest of the afternoon. Often a case can consume a person, and the brain begins to wear down. When this happens the smallest detail can easily slip past, and it can be easy to lose track of the trail, you are following. I was beginning to worry that Hannah's drive to find answers was tiring her out and she would miss something. I, on the other hand, was a trained professional and knew when I needed a little rest.

Walking south on East Bay Street, I passed a group of tourists standing outside of an oyster bar waiting for opening. I smiled at the power Food Network has on an establishment.

Charleston had become a restaurant destination, and each time a venue was featured on television it soon had a line out the door... great for business, but bad for locals who once enjoyed that particular bar or restaurant. About once a month a new bar or eatery would become the new tourist hotspot and Charlestonians would have to retreat and find a new location to unwind after work. It was the price you paid when living in a tourist mecca.

I crossed Broad Street and stared at the magnificent structure of 1 Broad. It was an old bank building, three stories high, and garnished with lion heads as keystones. The building, faced with brownstone, was designed in an Italian Renaissance style and seemed currently abandoned...odd for such a prime location and such an impressive historic structure. I stopped and stared for a bit and began to read a historical plaque attached to the side. The building, built in 1857, was heavily bombarded by Union artillery during the war. It was rebuilt in 1868 by...my mouth dropped as I read...George A. Trenholm. The fact led me to examine the structure further. It was a corner building facing both East Bay and Broad streets. Ornate and detailed craftsmanship could be seen on the outside and through the windows to the refined interior. The building did not seem in too bad of shape, and it only made me more curious as to why it was unoccupied.

On both street sides, there were secondary entrances that appeared to lead to the upper floors, and instead of sidewalk there was grating along the Broad Street side that gave view to the buildings foundation. Looking like a fool to those that passed by me I bent down to look through the grating. Nothing seemed out of place or different, but at the same time, I couldn't find the necessity of having grating instead of a typical sidewalk. I pulled out my phone and turned on my flashlight app. The shadows where the gray foundation met the brown stone lit up and I began to notice graffiti scratched into the surface. At first glance, it looked like something the construction workers left behind. Often when building significant structures, those who worked on its construction would leave something behind as a way to sign their craftsmanship. And, at first glance, that was all I saw.

My knees were bothering me, and I was about to stand up and move along when I noticed something that stood out. At the end bordering the main entrance, the northeast corner of the building, I saw it…the hooked x.

CHAPTER 43

My excitement was only overpowered by the pain in my knees from squatting the past five minutes. Before looking any further, I knew I had to let Hannah see what I found. I stood up and notice a man staring at me from across East Bay Street. In front of the Exchange Building was Tommy Makem. At first, he appeared like a man deep in thought, standing still and staring in my direction, but almost instantly he acknowledged that I saw him with a smile and a nod of his head before moving along south towards the Battery.

Was Makem following me? Probably not. He more than likely saw me squatting along the side of a building like an idiot and was curious. No matter, I had more important things to deal with at the moment.

"Hannah," I said into my phone. "What do you know about the building at 1 Broad Street?"

"Not much. Why?"

"Dig up what you can quickly and meet me here now," I said excitedly into the phone.

"What is it?" She asked with a voice that she was curious and a little nervous.

"I'd rather show you. Just get over here."

Within five minutes, I saw Hannah walking towards me on Broad with a tablet in front of her face. She walked with authority, hair bouncing with each step as her legs moved forward with great determination. She did not look up from her tablet once, as the usually clueless tourists moved to the side as she walked. It was like everyone sensed that Hannah was a woman on a mission.

"An impressive building," Hannah said when she got to where I stood on the front step of the structure. "I'm sure you saw the Trenholm connection, and that's why you called me?"

"No, that's what made me stop and look around. Look at this." I moved down off of the first step and knelt down again pointing below the grate. Hannah bent down next to me. "Do you see it?"

"See what?"

I turned my flashlight app on again. "How about now?"

"The hooked x."

We both stared for a few seconds, and a world of other objects appeared. I had previously been too blind to recognize them in my excitement. What I had earlier mistook for the carvings of construction workers now looked more like the tree in St. Phillip's Cemetery. Animals, letters, numbers, and other images appeared along the base of the building. They were so jumbled that with a quick glance it seemed like nothing at all, and without a flashlight, they would not have been visible in the shadows of the building and the sidewalk grate.

"What does it all mean?" I asked.

"There has to be another message her." Hannah turned the camera on her tablet towards the carvings. "Move your light along so I can get all this." She panned along with the light. "There is another clue here, but what? I don't see *J.A.M.* anywhere."

I stood, knees still in pain. "Why don't we go somewhere and look over the pictures slowly and try to match something up with what we already know. Besides, I feel awkward and sore bending over to look down a street grate."

"Good idea. Who knows who might be out here watching us too?"

Hannah's comment made me think back to Tommy Makem standing across the street. "You might be more right than you know. Come on, let's go to my place."

CHAPTER 44

It was a nondescript blue house, black shutters, and a red roof. The man standing across the street in front of the Carolina Yacht Club put out his cigarette with a frustrated twist of his ankle before crossing over to 53 East Bay Street. The house did not stand out when compared to the mansions that lined the street on the west side heading towards the Battery. Instead, the blinds were pulled, the front door was not in use and in need of some paint, and weeds grew up the north corner of the building. The man gave a glance up and down the sidewalk before entering a black iron gate, partially hidden from view, and adorned with a small sign that read: *The Charleston Club A.D. 1852.*

The man moved down the overgrown alley to the side door of the residence. A single gaslight was lit beside the entrance that signaled that the house was still occupied. Three knocks…a pause…three more knocks and the door swung open. An older gentleman answered, dressed in a black suit, and wore white gloves. The man at the door took his first two fingers and his thumb and moved them across his lips. The older gentleman waited a moment and then responded with a swipe of his thumb behind his ear.

"Please come in Mr. Makem." The older gentleman said.

"Thank you, Jefferson," Makem replied.

Jefferson, the butler, led Makem down a hall adorn with oil paintings of prominent members of the organization. The wood floors creaked below as they walked.

"Everyone else has arrived," Jefferson said, finally opening a door towards the end of the hallway. "Please ring if you need anything."

Makem entered the room, and Jefferson quietly closed the door behind him. In sharp contrast to the plain exterior of the house, the room was decorated elaborately and in elegant shape. The wood floors were polished and shimmered in the glow coming from the lights and the marble fireplace. Sky blue walls were adorned with golden framed paintings, and the windows and ceiling were outlined with thick white molding. The room ran the length of the house along its north side, with the exterior windows protected from prying eyes by the close proximity of the neighboring building. Large shrubs separated the two.

About a dozen men stood around, holding drinks and conversing quietly in small groups. Makem moved towards two men standing in front of the wet bar on the opposite end from the fireplace. He grabbed a glass at the bar, not looking towards the two men, and filled it with bourbon from a crystal decanter. As he finished his pour, a man walked in front of the fireplace.

"I believe we are all here." George Trenholm said in a voice that echoed across the room. "I now call to order this meeting of the Knights of the Golden Circle, protectors of the South, keepers of American beliefs, and charged with restoring the Union to its previous glory by the powers of Our Heavenly Father. Now everyone, please sit. We have an urgent matter to discuss."

The men began to move around to an array of seats in front of George Trenholm. Each man had a predetermined spot based on their place in the organization. Tommy Makem was not the highest ranking member, that position belonged to Trenholm, but he still held a prominent position and found his seat in the front of the group. The noise of a dozen men moving slowly petered off and the room once again became silent.

"I called you all here because we are under attack." Trenholm began. "We have enemies on two sides. I must take the blame for bringing one of them against us. The other is still a mystery to me. I will ask Mr. Makem to explain further."

Tommy Makem stood and walked toward Trenholm the two men nodded and then shook, Citadel rings sparkling from each man's hand. Trenholm took a seat and left Makem alone to address the people in the room.

"The first enemy Mr. Trenholm has spoken of is Jack Francis. He is a private investigator from Cleveland. Former FBI and an Army veteran. He is a worthy foe. Francis was hired to investigate the murder of Jason Trenholm and protect the family's history. Instead, his curiosity has gotten to him, and he has continued to look into the Trenholm past long after he has been dismissed by the family. Francis is working with a woman professor of Southern History from Columbia University. Her knowledge and drive for answers could be an enormous problem, possibly larger than Francis." Makem paused and tried to catch the feel of the room.

An older gentleman who was head of the South Carolina Savings & Loan spoke up. "What exactly is this Francis investigating?"

"Jason Trenholm was working with the professor during his graduate studies," Makem answered. "She created a curiosity in the young man to explore his family's past, and he eventually

155

discovered more than he was supposed to know at his age. I'm not sure how, but Francis and the professor have continued that research in the aftermath of Jason's mysterious death, and it led them to St. Phillip's Church, and on my walk here I saw Mr. Francis exploring 1 Broad Street."

The men throughout the room all expressed great concern with the news. Many reached for their drinks, while others squirmed in their chair.

"And what of the second enemy Mr. Trenholm spoke of?" Another man asked. He was young, energetic, and a promising first-term Senator.

"I believe, as does Mr. Trenholm, that whoever killed Jason did so because of his family's name. The death of Eliza Dunn confirmed this for me. I'm not sure why they were killed, but it's too coincidental, especially with Francis poking his nose around. Unlike Francis, I believe our second enemy may be an older one. Someone who knows Charleston, its families, and its history. Jason's murder was an obvious one, but Eliza Dunn took a little more thought."

There were murmurs around the room as the men talked the news over with those they sat next to. Finally, after a few minutes, George Trenholm stood and rejoined Makem at the front. The other men noticed and grew silent again.

"I have Mr. Makem dealing with these issues." Trenholm began. "I have only brought this to the attention of the group because of the significant risk it may have for us. I ask that each of you express your concerns or solutions to these problems because it is through the strength of each individual that we have succeeded in the past and how we will prosper in the future."

The men began to murmur again, and as opinions cultivated, the conversations grew louder. A man stood and surveyed the room, he glanced towards Trenholm and Makem at the front and then proceeded to the wet bar to refill his drink. He walked back and stood between the two men standing at the front and the group seated. Everyone went silent.

An air of respect filled the room as the man spoke. "We must find out how much Francis knows. We must discover our hidden enemy. And we must silence their curiosity by all means necessary."

The men of the group looked to the man they knew as their governor when he sat. Then they glanced to Trenholm waiting for a response. Trenholm didn't speak. Instead, a smile of satisfaction broke across his face. He knew that the group had now given him permission to use 'all means necessary.'

CHAPTER 45

"What's with the tablet?" I asked Hannah. Pouring some red wine into her glass while we sat on the porch.

"Not sure what you mean?"

"All of a sudden you can't put it down."

"Oh." She said slightly embarrassed. "When I first went to college I took a little notebook around with me everywhere. If I had a question I wanted to find the answer to I would write it down and then go to the library. I would write the answer down and then some of my own thoughts. The notebook would always be by my side in case I ever came up with a question I didn't want to forget. By the time I went to grad school laptops had become popular with the students, but I was so attached to my notebook that I couldn't let it go. Grad school was more of a challenge for me and opened up an array of avenues to explore. When I reached my final semester, I was carrying a messenger bag with three different notebooks in it."

"Wow, you were quite the nerd." I smiled.

Hannah gave me a smirk. "Anyways, while I was doing my doctorate laptops got lighter, and they finally began to weigh less than my notebooks, so I switched. It also helped that they finally became cheap enough for me to afford one. I enjoyed using the laptop, but I still needed notepads for my historical research…most of the historical documents at the time hadn't been uploaded to the web. About a two years ago Columbia, the University of Chicago, and a few other schools greatly expanded their online libraries."

"How so?" I asked, honestly curious.

"They provided access to previous students' thesis, dissertations, and studies resident instructors had done. Then the libraries at the schools joined with museums to create online databases for historical documents…old manuscripts, diaries, account books, and other pieces of history. Now these databases provide a vast amount of knowledge right at my fingertips. Columbia gave all of its professors these tablets to use in our studies and teachings, and now having all that information, along with ways to explore it, at the touch of a button is too hard to put down."

"Why are you spending so much time at the South Carolina Historical Society then?"

Hannah frowned a little. "Unfortunately, like most of this state, the Historical Society is stuck in the past and has yet to make their collection available online."

"So you are combining what you've found at their library with what we've discovered in the field and along with what's already online to create a picture of our investigations?"

"Exactly."

"I could get used to having one of those," I said pretending to reach for her tablet. She slapped my hand away. "It sounds like you are spending all of your time studying the past for an investigation today. I know there are historical connections, but what are you trying to find?"

"In history, there are clues to the present," Hannah said.

"I know, learn from history, or you're destined to repeat it."

"No, not quite. History doesn't repeat itself, but history does rhyme."

"Rhyme?"

Hannah smiled at my confusion. "A lot of history sounds the same. World War I and World War II, the American Revolution, and the French Revolution, and the work of Martin Luther King and Gandhi all sound alike, but when you dig deeper and try to define them it is easy to see that they are different. They sound the same but, in fact, have different meanings, causes, and effects."

"How does that correlate to us and our search for Confederate gold?"

"History has patterns because people are creatures of habit. You can use the past to interpret patterns and associate them with events of the present. It allows historians to predict future trends all while researching the historical events of civilization. It is the reason studying the subject is so significant."

I still wasn't figuring out how this all connected to our work. "What exactly does that mean for us?"

"It means I am searching for patterns in the history of the South, Charleston, the KGC, and the Trenholms looking for clues to help us resolve our current challenges…breaking the KGC code, finding out why Jason and Eliza were killed, and how are they all connected."

I sat back in my chair and swirled my wine a little for effect. "Sounds like a lot of work…let me know if you find anything." I closed my eyes, leaned my head back a little, and took a sip of wine. It was time to recharge the batteries.

CHAPTER 46

The tablet in Hannah's hand began to light up like the chalkboard scene in *A Beautiful Mind*. A photo of the marks and carvings on the foundation of 1 Broad Street was on the screen as Hannah highlighted objects with her finger. With a couple of taps, a half-dozen barely recognizable markings now illuminated to life creating a clearer picture of what was in front of us. A ghost, a ship, something that appeared to be a money sign, the letters *ISH*, a tree, and finally a symbol with numbers and dots.

"Out of all of these markings," Hannah said, "I believe these are our clues."

"How do you figure?"

"We've already seen the ghost used once and the cemetery theme has been consistent. The ghost here could simply be leading us back to St. Phillip's or to something new, but I believe it's important. The ship falls in line with the James' tombstones and their place as merchants. How exactly, I'm not sure, but it's not a coincidence. The fact that there is a money sign and these markings were placed on a bank building is also too much for me to believe in coincidence."

"What about the others?" I asked. "They seem new."

"They are, but there is only one of each carved into the building's foundation, while all the other symbols can be found multiple times."

"So you're saying their singularity is the way to identify what the real clue is and what is merely a ruse?"

"It's just a theory." Hannah stared at the screen as if she was trying to break it with her mind. "But I think it's a reliable one. I'm going out on a limb here, but just like with the letters *JAM* I believe the *ISH* symbolizes a name…Isaiah. Look here," she pointed to the last symbol, a mixture of numbers and dots. "The number twelve with for dots on either side."

"Another Bible verse?"

"I think so. It's either Isaiah 8:12 or Isaiah 44:12 from my best guess."

I quickly grabbed my phone and searched for the verses. "Say ye not, A confederacy, to all them to whom this people shall say, A confederacy; neither fear ye their fear, nor be afraid. Isaiah 8:12." I read out loud. "That's got to be it."

"Possibly, what does the other verse say?"

I glanced feeling I was right with the first one. The confederacy reference was just too perfect. "The smith with the tongs both worketh in the coals, and fashioneth it with hammers, and worketh it with the strength of his arms: yea, he is hungry, and his strength faileth: he drinketh no water, and is faint." I read to her.

"Okay, I'll need to keep both of those two in mind moving forward." Hannah was silent for a few moments. It was as if she was memorizing the verses. "I have to admit that these clues could be way off. There is just so much information to go through."

"Your reasoning seems right. Where should we go next? We have at least to try to prove your work correct."

"I have a couple of ideas. I've seen common themes in our search so far. The obvious one is the Trenholms. Second, and more recent, is the James family and their association as merchants. Third is death or burial sites. And fourth is the use of trees."

"Trees?" I asked.

"The tree in St. Phillip's Cemetery was the focal point of the clue there, and now we have a tree carved into the building. Also, the KGC were notorious for cutting clues and messages into trees. They were often known as 'wisdom trees' because of the information they held."

"Okay, how do we put it all together to locate our next spot? The first place we found because of Trenholm's letter. The second one we got lucky. It looks like the third will have to be a combination of both."

"Good research always trumps luck," Hannah said.

"I still won't turn down a little luck if it comes a calling."

CHAPTER 47

The strangest thing that had struck me recently, and lately I was stumbling on a lot of strange things, was the fact that there had been zero outcries from the South of Broad neighborhood over the murders. In a community with zero crime rate to suddenly have two deaths, especially two of its own, usually called for a public outcry. The local police would usually have their hands full dealing with the case and the public at the same time. Instead, everything seemed quiet.

The paper lacked any updates on a suspect, and it was almost like there was no investigation currently in progress. In fact, Eliza's husband had been written off because of an alibi, but there was no mention of other suspects. In my experience, when an investigation was kept quiet someone powerful had their hands in it. The fact that the neighborhood where the murders took place was equally silent left me to believe that same person had a real stranglehold on the neighbors as well.

Hannah had gone off to lecture at the college, and I was stuck going through all the information we had collected. I was focusing in on the Trenholm and James families, somewhere there was a connection, or was the connection simply that their gravestones had been the perfect spot to leave clues to a lost treasure? I found that the James family had been around Charleston, in a position of power, a lot longer than the Trenholms. Apparently, the Trenholm family didn't amount to much until George A. Trenholm made his fortune prior to the Civil War while the elder James had ties to the city's founding.

The eldest James had gone into business with Christopher Gadsden, father of the 'Don't Tread on Me' flag, post-American Revolution. They helped finance Gadsden's Wharf's reconstruction after the British left the city, and shortly thereafter made an enormous fortune by contributing to the importation of over one-hundred-thousand slaves into the country through Charleston. It appeared after 1808 that the James family removed their ties to the wharf, which happened to be the same point Fraser & Company, pre-Trenholm, began leasing warehouse and dock space there. It wasn't much to go on, but it at least it was a connection.

I searched other information on the two families finding no similarities, except that each was extensive landowners with holdings in plantations, homes in the city, and business properties. The curious thing was the James family had a lot of information about them pre-Civil War, but that all ended with James III. It was as if the war began and all records for the family stopped. I couldn't even find an obituary for the youngest James or if he had any offspring. It was as if the family stopped existing. There was zero information on what happened to their holdings. I found the information on one of their plantations that had survived General Sherman and his men, but there were no ownership records during the period of Reconstruction. It appeared that a northern carpetbagger had merely taken up residence after the war, and eventually his family sold it as their own to a New York firm looking for a hunting retreat in the 1950s.

Dead-end searches and investigative research makes me hungry, so I printed out what lists I could find of properties owned by the Trenholms and James families. I tucked the printed pages into a pocket along with my cell phone and decided to find some food. I promised myself I would continue my work over a cold beer, and smartphone technology would provide the means. I texted Hannah to have her join me but got no immediate response. Deep down inside, I was hoping to pass the dirty work off to her…she was better at it than me.

I was talking to Colin on my cell phone as I walked north on King St. My former FBI partner was obviously bored at the office. If he were sincerely interested in how my work in Charleston was going, I would be surprised. I had made it to the corner of King and Society when I suddenly stopped. There in the back of my head was the feeling that I was being followed.

It's an odd feeling, and I'm not sure where it comes from, but one minute you're in your own little world on a busy street and then suddenly you feel like someone is staring a lightning bolt through your back.

I kept talking to Colin, but looked up at the street sign and then turned to look down Society Street. I wanted to make it look like I was looking for something and not someone. I wanted to make whoever was following me believe the person on my phone was giving me directions. Making some hand gestures as I talked, I finally turned around some more to get a look at the crowd behind me on King. Nothing. Turning further, and now fixing my gaze across the street to the opposite sidewalk, I tried to recognize anyone the least bit suspicious. There was nothing still. I held my stare for a few seconds longer hoping to grasp something I had missed, and I did. In the doorway of a woman's boutique stood a man. It wasn't the cross-armed boredom of a husband waiting for his wife, but instead the goonish stance of Tommy Makem.

CHAPTER 48

Walking up King St. a couple blocks with my tail in tow, I slipped through a crowd of shoppers into a chicken wing joint on the street's west side. The bar sat street side, and I could get a good view of the crowds passing by as I drank a beer. There was no sign of Makem, as I ordered a Holy City Porter from the bartender. Either he saw me and ducked into a restaurant, or he was waiting outside. By the time the bartender poured the pint and set it down in front of me with a menu in hand, Tommy Makem had come trudging up the sidewalk with a pissy look for every tourist that bumped into him. He turned to glance through the windows, and we made eye contact. I smiled. He nodded and came inside.

"What have I done to deserve such an honor?" I asked, as Makem sat and motioned for the bartender.

"Oh, I was doing a little window shopping."

"Bullshit. I spotted you following me blocks ago."

Makem squirmed in his seat a little. "I'm going to give it to you straight Francis. Partly, because I like you and partly because we come from the same town, but mostly because a warning is only fair. There are some powerful people in this city. They've run this city for hundreds of years, saved it from the ruin caused during Reconstruction by making it a tourist town, and today they are more desperate than ever to hold onto their control."

"Why's that?" I asked.

"Because of people like you and I. Northerners who have seen how beautiful Charleston is and want a piece of it for themselves. The old bluebloods who run the show here want our tourist dollars, but would rather see us leave after a week than stay permanently. There is a new generation of carpetbaggers in their eyes."

"So why do I need a warning? I'm only here temporarily."

"You're butting your nose in where it doesn't belong. You and that the teacher are getting a little too curious about the local history around here, and some critical people are getting upset. These aren't merely influential businessmen, but the kind of individuals that can make problems disappear if needed. You know the type?"

"Tell me Makem, how have you found yourself involved? Why are you, a fellow Yankee, passing along a warning to me?"

The man paused, barely, and most people wouldn't have noticed, but I did. "I've got business ties to these people, and they knew we'd been talking. I was approached to keep an eye on you and send a message if needed. There is no need for me to follow you around all day and waste my time if I can only pass the message along...so that's what I'm doing."

There was more Makem wasn't telling me, and that fact was a big clue. I wanted to find a connection. Originally, Makem was a separate entity in this case, but now the pieces may be falling together a little better. I only needed to figure out the link.

"I'm not buying it," I said to Makem. "Why is a little historical research so threatening to these people?"

"People in Charleston take their history more seriously than anywhere else. Their status and position in society depends on what history says about their family. Sometimes, what history says and what the history actually is aren't always the same."

"So you're saying if the real history is discovered it could possibly affect the livelihood of someone?" I asked.

"A little change in the history might affect the livelihood of someone in this town, a significant change could impact multiple families."

Makem got up and threw some cash on the bar for his drink.

"I've got that," I said, handing the money back to him. "I can't imagine what could be so important to these people."

"At the end of the day, it's all about the same thing…money." Makem walked to the door and stopped before he stepped out. "You've been warned, Francis. These Southerners will be sweet to your face all day long, but that's just a devilish ruse to hide their mean streak."

CHAPTER 49

"We've been warned," I said to Hannah, as I spread my research across her kitchen counter.

It was actually the first time I had been to her place, and it was sterile, immaculate, and the opposite of cozy. She was renting the top floor of a building on King Street, and it had been remodeled in the loft-modern style that provides zero personality to a home. The elevator had opened into an open space that spanned the entire third floor. Hardwood floors ran left to right, with bright open windows to my left that let in light and the noise from the street below. In front of me stood the kitchen with granite counters, stainless steel appliances, and cabinetry that looked like it came from an Ikea store. Off to my right, through a dining space, were two doors that I could only assume lead to the bedroom and bath. I was already missing the old hardwood, exposed brick, and two-hundred-year-old fireplaces of my carriage house.

"What do you mean?" Hannah asked.

"I spotted Tommy Makem tailing me today. He finally had enough of the game and stopped to talk. Apparently, we are pissing off some very influential local boys with our snooping."

"How's Tommy connected?"

"I'm not sure, but they sent him after us with the message."

"The Citadel."

"What about it?" I asked confused.

Hannah looked excited. "Makem went to the Citadel. The Charleston aristocracy sends their young men to either Sewanee in Tennessee or to the Citadel here in Charleston. The connection must be during his time at the Citadel. Makem must have made connections there with some of the locals, built up his ties to the bookie business, and it appears got involved in some kind of secret group."

"A secret group like the Knights of the Golden Circle?"

"Possibly. He would have had really to prove himself as an outsider and particularly since Makem is a Northerner."

"In my experience people who use the same bookie over an extended period usually have built confidence in that person. When you trust someone with your money, finances, and especially debt you'll have faith in them with about anything. If Makem were college friends with these men, the trust would have come a lot quicker."

Hannah stood quietly for a moment locked in thought and then turned to see the mess of papers I had spread over her counter. "What's all this?"

"My research."

"Well organized." She said with a smile and a hint of sarcasm. "What did you find?"

I began to organize my work. "Not a lot. I've gathered all the records I could find that might connect the James Family with the Trenholms. The only obvious connection, and it's a stretch, was the Gadsden Wharf. I also mapped out all known properties the two families had an interest in throughout the area. The hope was to find a connection or joint ownership...nothing there, though."

"Why is there nothing for the James Family after the Civil War?" Hannah asked.

"There was nothing for me to find. It was as if the family had been wiped off the face of the Earth during the war."

"Interesting," Hannah said as she began to pilfer through my work.

Bent over with elbows on the granite counter top, Hannah shuffled papers and organized the pages to suit her needs. Her hair was in a ponytail with one loose strand dropping in front of her left eye. Hannah kept tucking it back behind her ear only to have it fall again. I watched the battle between her and her hair for a few moments thinking how much easier it would be simply to redo her ponytail, but I was a guy, so what did I know?

Hannah stood up, cocked her head and looked at me for a moment. She then bit her thumbnail and walked back into the bedroom. A few seconds later she came out with her trusty tablet. The scrolling went on for a couple minutes as her fingers hurriedly stroked the screen of the electronic device. When they stopped, she read, looked at the papers spread along the counter, read from the tablet again, and finally looked up at me with a smile.

"Come over here." She said to me.

I walked to her side of the counter and followed her lead as she bent over a map of the Charleston region I had used to mark properties. Hannah reached for a pen and began to make marks across the Charleston peninsula and finally connected them with a couple lines.

"What do you see?" She asked.

I looked over the map. "A cross."

CHAPTER 50

"I know what you're thinking," Hannah said. "Anyone can pick points on a map and draw a cross, but look here." Hannah pulled the tablet up and produced a document that appeared to be a scholarly paper.

"From your professor friend at Columbia?"

"Yes." She said. "Now, he proposed that the KGC used a series of symbols that when laid across a map could pinpoint the location of a hidden cash. The first step was to pinpoint markers in the area and then put the symbol on the map trying to line up the markers with points on the symbol."

"We've only found two markers, and one of those doesn't even line up with your cross." I wasn't too optimistic at this point.

"The first indicator, St. Phillip's, was a keystone or a map to the actual markers. 1 Broad Street is a real guide. You mentioned that Gadsden's Wharf held a connection to the Trenholms and the James Family. Well, it lines up with my cross, and now happens to be named Liberty Square. Home to the Fort Sumter Visitors Center and the boats that take you to the fort."

"It does have a certain intrigue to it. What are the other points?" I asked.

"The first is Ashley Hall School, an all-girl academy here on the peninsula. The reason I am confident about this marker is that the original building for the school once belonged to George A. Trenholm…it was once his home in the city. The second location is Magnolia Cemetery where the man is buried."

I paused at the thought. These locations made sense, but Hannah also seemed to be grasping at the obvious. Doubtful, I looked at the map and then at her.

"These locations seem too obvious, minus Liberty Square, and are we supposed to just dig for buried treasure where the lines of the cross intersect?"

"That's the basic idea, but no. The lines intersect in a residential area with no real connection to Trenholm, or the James Family for that matter. We need to confirm these spots as markers and look for further clues. Hopefully, I'm right and somewhere there is a clue to the final location."

"I'm game, but it's because we haven't got much else. I'm not questioning your research techniques or your theory, but I've learned not to be optimistic this early on. Something always goes wrong or we'll find we've missed something obvious along the way."

Hannah smiled. "I'm aware that I'm grasping, but a lot of it makes sense. Besides, it won't hurt to go and look, and if I'm wrong, we will know soon enough."

"Okay, we'll start the hunt tomorrow. Which spot do you want to hit first?"

"The square, then the school, and then we will save the cemetery for last."

"Why's that?" I asked.

"I believe there is an order that needs to be followed and finding the ship carved into 1 Broad Street leads me to believe that we are supposed to go to the wharf next. When we get there, it may point us somewhere else, or we may find nothing at all."

"Why are we doing this again?"

"What do you mean?" Hannah asked, perplexed by my question.

"Why are we still following up on this? I was fired by Trenholm, threatened by Makem and a group of unknown men, and I'm wondering why we are still pushing forward?"

"To find out what secrets are worth the price of two individuals' lives. Plus, I feel responsible for bringing Jason into this mess. If I hadn't taken him on as my graduate assistant, had him research his own family, and push him to find answers he might still be alive. He definitely wouldn't have gone through the books in his father's study and found that letter, which seems to be what set this whole mess off."

"And I feel the need to provide Bryce some answers into his friend's death, so we march forward into the unknown…and hopefully, don't wind up dead ourselves." I said.

CHAPTER 51

Elliott Tidwell drove a beat up Ford F-250 south on Highway 17. The truck, born in the seventies, was all white, speckled with rust, and missing the tailgate. It rumbled along on oversized tires that increased the noise in the cab as it struggled to maintain the sixty miles an hour speed limit. Tidwell had the windows down, and his thin squirrelly hair blew about as he scanned the radio.

Charleston is a mini-metropolis surrounded by rivers, estuaries, creeks, and swamps all along the coast and west to Orangeburg. There are thousands of undisturbed acres where civilization is scarce and nature and history rule. There are small communities of blacks tucked into isolated areas, where they have been since Emancipation. Work is limited, and they never venture far from the plantations that once held them captive. Here, like most of the South is a contrast of life. While these small black enclaves struggled to survive another group sat as symbols of Southern power. Tucked along the banks of rivers, down long drives, and guarded with Spanish moss covered oaks were some of the wealthiest landowners in the South. Not all plantations remained after the Civil War, but many did. Much of the Carolina Lowcountry was spared by Sherman's torch and lived on as working farms, hunting grounds, and tourist attractions. Most families that owned plantation homes did everything they could to hold on to their enduring symbol of the Old South.

The drive south along Highway 17 took Tidwell across the Edisto River, the Ashepoo, and through the ACE Basin. He was deep into plantation country. After a little more than a fifty-mile drive he turned right onto White Hall Road, a narrow piece of pavement that wound its way through the pristine forest, an old colonial church, barns long unused, and unmarked driveways. He continued until he came to Combahee Road and turned. Here the pavement narrowed further to one lane as he began to cross creeks, marshes, and abandoned rice fields on flimsy made bridges and earthen dams. The forest retreated leaving the land speckled with small brush, palmetto trees, and large live oaks.

Almost fifteen minutes after he turned off of Highway 17, Tidwell veered into a dirt drive marked only by a brick and wrought iron gate. There was no sign and no indication of what lay down the drive. The drive wound through the vegetation following a creek, as it made its way to the Combahee River. Deer scattered at the sound of the old truck and nature briefly retreated as it bounced along the dirt road. The creek split from the drive after a mile and the canopy above and around Tidwell opened to a field. On the right side, broken fencing marked once used grazing areas, and four abandoned cabins on the left hinted at the slaves once housed in them. Oak trees lined the drive, but some were missing and others sickly. The trees, the slave cabins, and the broken fence all spoke of history and grandeur, but the reality resembled a ghost town.

The truck chugged along kicking up dust as it moved towards the house on the river's bluff. Chips were missing from the siding's whitewash and the black shutters hung loosely closed. Tidwell pulled around what once was a fountain and parked the truck along the side of the home. He got out and reached back into the vehicle to grab his sword and a small bag from the passenger seat. Instead of going to the front of the house with its main entrance now rotting away, he moved to the back entering through a servant's door. There, inside, was the home's kitchen. Tidwell set down his belongings on the table and immediately began a pot of coffee. There was work to be done, and he understood the terrible blow his objectives took when he messed up his confrontation with Francis. He must recharge, reexamine, and organize himself. Failure was not an option this time.

The coffee pot began to churn, and Tidwell got a cup from one of the cabinets. He knew that the professor was holding on to the letter, but Francis was always by her side. Somehow he needed her alone. He needed to have her all to himself and then she would tell him where the letter was, or better yet where it would lead him. *If only*, he thought…*If only he could get her all the way out here.*

CHAPTER 52

Liberty Square is on the northern edge of Charleston's historic district and borders the Cooper River. On the north side of the square lies the Charleston Aquarium, an old theater and some offices, and to the south is the Fort Sumter Welcome Center. A large park-like setting sits in between with a grand entrance gate littered with tourists taking pictures while waiting for the boats out to the fort. Hannah and I had taken a pedicab and paid the driver in cash, with a hefty tip, before beginning our exploration of the area.

My initial thought was that we were in the wrong place. The large square was mostly open space covered with grass, a few benches, and even fewer monuments. If there were a clue here, one covered in markings, someone would have surely noticed it by now.

"Split up," I suggested to Hannah.

"Good idea."

We began to move in opposite directions. I went south, and she went north. There was one path that ran the outer ring of the square and one that crossed through diagonally, so I began to

181

walk the outer ring and figured we would meet in the middle. I took my time walking past the metal fence with the word *square* scrawled into it, but the wall looked too new, and I didn't find a thing. In fact, the whole square looked too new with most of the fencing, benches, and even the landscaping all seemingly added recently. I needed to find something with a little age on it.

I walked past a large cemented area that led to the Fort Sumter Welcome Center. There was a large brick pavilion filled with picnic tables and outlined with flag poles sporting the Stars and Stripes. I walked around the welcome center, taking care to examine the foundation, stairs, and even underneath where access was available. The brick structure was newly constructed and turned out to be the dead end I expected.

I moved towards the aquarium along the water and watched a water taxi bob up and down in its floating dock. I knew the aquarium was new and thought I would pass on checking it out, but I knew Hannah wouldn't approve that approach. It took me twenty minutes to examine the building, all with the watchful eyes of their old security guard on me, only to find nothing. When I was done, I had spent almost an hour of my life walking around half the square for nothing. Heading towards the path that led diagonally through the grass I noticed that I couldn't see Hannah. She had been easy to follow across the open space but appeared to have disappeared. I stopped and looked towards the theater and the office buildings hoping she would materialize shortly.

With five more minutes of my life wasted, I finally decided to go look for her myself. Walking past the aquarium towards the theater, I realized that there was a larger and older dock area that emerged before you got to the office building. At the edge where cement met the dock, I noticed Hannah. She stood perfectly still and had her hand shading her eyes from the sun. The wind coming up the harbor from the ocean blew strands of her ponytail in mismatched directions. I yelled to her, but my words were blown away by the incoming sea breeze.

"What's got you so entranced?" I asked, approaching her from behind. She jumped slightly startled.

"What? Oh, sorry you startled me."

"What's got your attention?"

Hannah changed her startled face to one that appeared to start a class lecture, firm and thoughtful. "Once upon a time this was the main dock area for Gadsden's Warf."

"How do you know?"

"See how many of those large pieces of wood are sticking out from the water?"

"Yeah, they look like supports."

"They are. See how the posts extend into the river in rows. That and their size tell me they once supported large working docks at one time. Also, this is premium docking space, but when they built a new marina for the square they did so on the other side of the aquarium. Typical of Charleston's style, they tried to preserve some aspect of history here."

I thought it over for a moment. "Why protect simple dock posts, which at the very least represented a dark part of Charleston history…the slave trade?"

"I agree. That's why I was looking so intently. Why preserve rotting dock posts? Unless there was some importance or something important they still held."

I began to stare with her scanning each individual post the best I could. The sun was causing glare and making it difficult.

"We may need a boat," Hannah said.

"Hold on," I said, looking at something I hadn't noticed before.

Boulders fashioned a barrier between the river and the office building's foundation. They created a wall extending along the water's edge of the building but then turned out into the river in the form of a breakwall. I began to climb out onto the rocks.

"What are you doing?" Hannah blurted.

"Going out there," I said pointing out to the breakwall.

"I'm going too."

Hannah climbed down behind me onto the scrawny rock wall. There was not enough room to walk on top, so we shimmied along the side with the building's concrete in our face and the waters of the Cooper River grasping at us from below. Movement was slow as I grasped for rock edges that hurt my hands and foot holes that didn't really exist. I slipped a couple times thinking that soon brackish water would be surrounding me. Hannah, on the other hand, ascended like a pro.

The rock wall finally turned into the breakwall, and I eagerly leaped to its top, and even though the walk was uneven, it was better than hanging on the side of sharp stones. Hannah and I moved slowly down the pseudo pier as we checked out each wood support we came across. Most were severely rotten, and if something had been carved into one the salt water would have removed it long ago.

"No one would have carved a clue onto these old dock supports. See how rotten and worn they are?"

"Yeah, you're probably right," Hannah said. "It's just that they are the only old thing in this whole square."

I kept walking down the length of the breakwall paying less attention to the old supports. Finally, I reached the end finding a sturdy spot to stand and looked out over the river. A freighter was making its way under the Ravenel Bridge, a beautifully constructed suspension bridge that opened in 2005. Charleston was an old and historic city, but all around there were signs of its recent growth.

"Jack," Hannah said.

"Where do we go from here?" Sincerely asking the question, while also quoting a title from work by Dr. King. Knowing how many Africans were brought in from the very spot I was standing had me a little caught up in the power of the moment.

"Look down."

I noticed Hannah was smiling as I took my gaze from the bridge and down to my feet. "Son of a bitch," I said.

A flat rock, the one I was standing on, was covered in markings. It was two by two-foot square and to my astonishment in perfect shape. It was the only cut stone on the breakwall and would have to have been replaced every once in a while, because of erosion from incoming waves, but there it was below my feet and covered with very familiar markings.

CHAPTER 53

"The stone was recently replaced, or the carvings were redone," Hannah said as she snapped pictures with her phone. "The rocks are sturdy and would put up a fight with the brackish waves, but if this were laid at the same time the carvings at 1 Broad were done, then they would have been a lot more worn."

I stood back watching her work and giving her some room on the tiny breakwall. The water taxi was leaving from the other side of the aquarium hauling tourists over to Patriots Point. No one cared or even seemed to notice the two people at the end of a rocky outcropping. I smiled at the thought of tourists and that tunnel vision trait they all possess.

"All right, let's go." Hannah stood and approached me. "I've got enough pictures. I'll start uploading them to my Cloud file and view them on the tablet when we get back. That way I can compare them with the other sites."

"Why don't we head over to that school you pegged as another location? We've got some momentum, and you seem to be spot on with your theory."

"I'm turning you into a believer," Hannah said with a smile. "We can't go waltzing onto the grounds of a private girls' school. When we get back to dry land, I'll make a call and see if we can't obtain permission to do our snooping."

The two of us slowly took the unsteady walk back to the edge of the office building and then climbed down on the rock wall for our awkward crossing back to the square. I moved first, and Hannah followed right behind me. Her smaller hands and feet seemed to make the sideways climb a little easier for her. About halfway across, with the river water nipping at my feet, I heard an echoed pop and suddenly rock sprayed from in between the two of us.

"What the hell was that?" Hannah yelled out.

I paused, afraid to move but also thinking about simply pushing myself off and back into the water.

"Gunshot," I said quickly. "Move."

I was expecting the kill shot to follow, and we were easy targets clinging awkwardly to the rocks. I was reaching and pulling my body sideways as fast as I could when the second shot hit to my left, taking away the rocks that would have been my next grab point. Frozen to the wall, I waited again. That second shot was close, but if someone wanted to hit us, it should have been easy. These were warning shots. I turned my head slowly towards the river. The water taxi was now halfway across the river, but no one on board would have noticed a shooter anyways. Turning my head as far as it could to the left, I ran out of room before I could see where the shots had come from. I changed directions and looked across my right shoulder. About a thousand feet out was a small center console with a solo outboard and a stack of crab traps in the back. One man stood at the wheel and another knelt at the bow with a rifle resting on the rail. The man at the rail caught me looking from his scope and gave a wave. The gun was lowered back into the boat, and he sat up signaling to his counterpart. With a struggled roar, the outboard surged the vessel forward and off towards the shallows of Shutes' Folly.

With the roar of the engine moving away from us, I began to work my way towards the shore again. Hannah, a little shaken, started to follow without a word.   Within minutes, I was back on the concrete at the edge of the square helping Hannah up with my left hand.

"Warning shots," I said.

"Yeah, but from whom?"

"Probably from Makem's boys."

"Or the Civil War enthusiast that broke into your place," Hannah said.

"No, these were Makem's people or at least relations of those he works for."

"How do you figure?"

"The stranger, Elliott Tidwell I think he called himself, is a loner. There is no significant organization or partner with him. I've seen his kind before when I was still at the Bureau. Makem, on the other hand, has always worked for, and obviously, still does, people with money. These people hire out, so they don't get their hands dirty."

"Makes sense. So, what now?"

"You call that school and get us permission to snoop," I said.

"After that?" Hannah said, unsure of my choice. "I was just shot at...a drink sounds more reasonable."

"Especially now, they believe that we've been warned off for today. Chances are we won't be followed to the school. First work and then I'll get you that drink."

CHAPTER 54

Hannah made of few phone calls. First to the head of her department at the College of Charleston and then to someone at Ashley Hall. The obvious ruse was that a distinguished Columbia professor wanted to tour the historic McBee House for research. We were given a three o'clock appointment and were greeted at the main gate by a young blonde woman. She introduced herself as Grace, a senior at the school, and wore a uniform typical of private institutions. Grace was a lanky girl, almost as tall as I was, and seemingly a bit awkward. I guessed she didn't have a lot of attention from the opposite sex yet, but she seemed smart, quick, and maybe opportunistic.

"Dr. Welsh," Grace said to Hannah. "When the office told me you wanted a tour of McBee House I volunteered right away."

"Why's that?" I asked, with a smirk.

"Excuse my associate, Grace. This is Mr. Francis, and we are doing some research together."

"Nice to meet you, Mr. Francis. To answer your question, I wanted to meet Dr. Welsh. I've read some of her work and am heading to Columbia next year."

"Wow, that's impressive," I said.

"You sound a little like me," Hannah said, with a soft smile for the young lady. "Now, why don't you give me the grand tour and explain every little tidbit you can about McBee House for me."

We began to walk from the main gate across the campus, passing a few students and a small building made of shells.

Grace caught me looking at the structure. "That's the Shell House, but you could've probably guessed that. It was built as an aviary. Charlestonians were once really into exotic birds…a sign of their wealth, I'm told. It's been a classroom, but now seniors use it as an escape from the underclassmen."

Moving along the paved path. we began to come upon a stately manor. Two stories of brick painted white, and a high basement allowed the mansion to tower over the open space below. A portico, supported by four massive columns, topped a large glass arch on the basement level. Within the central portico, on the second floor, was a large balcony decorated with black wrought iron."

"McBee House," Grace said.

"Impressive," I said, stopping and getting a better look.

The young woman began her well prepared tour moving us closer to the structure. "The McBee House, named after our founder Mary Vardine McBee, was built around 1816 for Patrick Duncan and it is assumed that the architect was the notable William Jay. The next owner, James Nicholson, purchased the house and surrounding grounds in 1829 and the home was named for him until it was changed to the McBee House. Other notable owners were James R. Pringle a South Carolina politician and George A. Trenholm Secretary of Treasury for the Confederate States of America."

I gave Hannah a smile as we move into the home from a door on the basement level below the portico.   It opened into a room, bright from the sun that came through the wall of glass behind us. In its modern form, it was a waiting area with chairs, magazines, a drinking fountain, and an older woman at plugging away on an aged computer.

"Hi, Mrs. Lambert." Grace said walking up to the desk. "May I have two visitor passes? I've giving a tour."

Mrs. Lambert smiled to her and pulled to clip-on passes from a drawer. Hannah and I soon had them clipped to our chest, and we moved to the interior of the mansion with Grace.

Grace began her rehearsed tour again. "We are in what is called the basement level of the house. It is now used for administrative offices, counselors, and student aides."

"Can we look into any of these rooms?" I asked as we walked down a central hallway.

"I'm sorry, but I'm not authorized to enter with tours. The top two floors are open though, and you should be able to get a good look around."

"Grace, what can you tell us about the basement? Any good historical facts or even rumors?" Hannah asked.

"There's really not much said about it. Most of the attention is always paid on the main floors. From what I've been told the basement was used for storage and servant quarters before the kitchen was moved down here after the War Between the States."

"Storage? Like food, wine, and stuff like that?" I asked.

"No, mostly for furniture. Most Antebellum families would have a rotation of furniture for the seasons. Food would be stored in the kitchen house, and wine was stored in a private room off of the study. I believe it was put in so the men could move into the study after dinner and drink without anyone keeping track of how much they had." Grace giggled a little at the thought.

We began to walk up the stairs to the main floor.

"Who put the private room in the study?" Hannah asked.

"I'm not sure. The house had many owners, and they all added unique little touches over the years. Mrs. McBee had run the school here for forty years before it was discovered."

"Really, that's interesting," Hannah said, glancing at me.

CHAPTER 55

The main floor was impressive, but I was beginning to be watered down by the opulence of old Charleston homes. A hall ran down the middle split by a broad stairway that curved up to the second floor. The floor was a beautifully polished hardwood, and walls painted a light blue and lined with oil paintings in gilded frames traveled twelve feet into the air. Light shone in from windows placed at both the front and back of the hall symmetrical to each other, and I had to guess duplicated on the second floor because of the natural light coming down the staircase. There were four doors in the hall residing in each of the mansion's four corners.

"The rooms," Grace began, "are now used for social functions. The school is a non-profit and holds fundraisers and ceremonies for the students here." She opened the first door on our left. "This room is the grand ballroom and extends the full length of the house. There is another entrance on the far end. During Gala Season, guests would be greeted at the front of the home and enter through the opposite door. The doorway we came through would be used by the servants to bring in food and drinks from the kitchen house out back."

The room was long and illuminated once again by natural light from large windows at either end. Within the windows were carved natural seating areas that I had seen before in ballrooms, and knew that under these benches were storage for table settings and other necessary items. The floor here was also perfectly polished hardwood, but the walls were done in an elaborate paper, speckled with sophisticated designs of pink and white. Thick molding in white towered above us and around the windows and two chandeliers hung from the ceiling. A fireplace adorned the middle of the outside wall along the length of the house.

The front room on the opposite side of the hall had been a parlor or sitting area, and the room to the rear of that was now a modern kitchen. Grace informed us that it once was the family's dining room. We marched upstairs to find three former bedrooms now used as offices, which we had been allowed to poke our heads in because the occupants were apparently on a field trip with the freshman class.

The final room on the second floor, in the front of the house and overlooking the quad below, was the original study. Mrs. McBee had apparently used it as her headmaster's office. Now it remained empty out of respect. Wood floors were covered with oriental carpets, and oak bookshelves lined the walls. A desk, large enough to stop a rhino, sat at the far end and was plainly decorated with writing equipment and a lamp. There was no sign of modern necessities, no phone or computer, and the lamp looked like it had seen better days.

Hannah gazed around at the bookshelves as Grace continued to talk. I walked behind the desk, examined its view of the room and then turned to look out the window behind it. Sun glistened on the trees but barely made it through to the grass because of dense coverage of the old oak, magnolia and crepe myrtles. I could see an older black man in blue overalls trimming hedges in the garden.

"Grace" Hannah turned from the bookshelf and interrupted the girl mid-sentence. "You mentioned a private room where wine was stored?"

"Yes." She said. "The wall between here and the interior wall is thicker than everywhere else in the house. It's hard to tell by the illusion created by the bookshelves. But I can show you."

Grace closed the door to the room and showed us how thick it was from where the door shut to where the edge of the bookshelves began.

"Mrs. McBee never noticed because she apparently always had the door open." Grace reopened the door and then moved towards the end of the bookshelves by the desk. She reached for a brown leather book and pulled it out. Behind was a latch that pulled a door open. "John Calhoun's *Disquisition on Government*. William Piper, who followed Mrs. McBee, thought it was odd that a one-hundred-page treatise would be in a leather bound book two inches thick. That's how the room was discovered. In fact, the cover is fake, and the actual text inside is a collection of treatises by John Locke."

"That's fascinating." Stated Hannah.

The lanky Grace opened the door and stepped back so we could look inside. The opening was barely large enough for one person and inside the space opened only slightly more to gain access to the floor to ceiling wine racks. There was a small ladder attached to the wall opposite the entranceway in order to reach bottles at the top of the rack.

"Like everything else in the study the wine room was left as it was found when Mrs. McBee retired. I assume that means it is still how it was when the last owner of the house used it since Mrs. McBee didn't know it existed." Grace was standing back with a smile at what she felt had been a successful tour.

I looked in the semi-dark space but couldn't see anything that would lead me to believe a KGC clue was hidden here. Hannah stepped in next and immediately climbed up the ladder a few steps. Grace tried to stop her, but Hannah didn't listen to the student. I couldn't see what Hannah was doing as half her body was now blocked from my view. There was some rustling around, as Grace continued to ask her to get down. A moment late I saw Hannah reach into her back pocket and remove her cell phone. Flashes began to illuminate the tiny wine closet sporadically for about a minute before Hannah climbed back down.

"What were you taking pictures of?" Grace asked.

"There were some really rare bottles up there I wanted to document," Hannah responded quickly. "Thanks for the tour Grace, but I think Mr. Francis and I have seen enough."

Hannah began to head for the door, and I followed. Grace tried to get us to wait as she shut the door to the wine closet and returned the book to its spot on the shelf. We were halfway down the stairs before the girl caught up.

"Wait," Grace called out sternly. We both stopped surprised that she had it in her. "I need to escort you both off the grounds. We are not allowed to have visitors unattended."

Hannah and I allowed the girl to take the lead and show us out. We said quick goodbyes, and Grace said she looked forward to seeing Hannah at Columbia in the fall.

"Did you find it?" I asked, leaving the school behind and turning the corner onto Rutledge Avenue.

"Sure did."

"How? I didn't see a thing while I was in there."

"You wouldn't have, because up close didn't give you the view needed. Standing back, I noticed a hooked x carved into one of the middle rungs of the ladder. That's why when you let me in there I knew I had to climb. Above the door, on the inside of the wine closet hung a cross, and on that cross were all the usual KGC markings." Hannah said.

"What now?"

"I still need that drink. I don't know if you remember, but we were shot at today."

"We'll get you that drink then. Probably could use one myself."

We walked back down Rutledge toward Calhoun heading towards King Street and Hannah's place. Her all-important tablet was there, and she wanted it before we did anything else. As we walked, I began to get that feeling again. The one I felt when Tommy Makem was following me. I turned to look a few times but saw nothing. Maybe it was my nerves getting to me. Having been shot at would put just about anyone on edge, but the feeling was too strong to ignore. I would have to keep a closer eye on my surroundings from here on out.

CHAPTER 56

Across the street from Hannah's place was a small Asian bar called CO. We sat, order some steam buns and dumplings, and a bottle of unoaked chardonnay. The moment the bartender poured the wine Hannah had the glass to her lips. She set the glass down, took a deep breath with her eyes closed, and then pulled out her tablet.

"Before you get started, maybe we should re-think things," I said.

"If you think someone shooting at us is going to put me off you're wrong. Honestly, if someone is that afraid of us then it makes me want to know what they're hiding even more."

"I agree, but I figured it was my duty to ask before we dug ourselves any deeper."

Letting Hannah work, I sat silently for twenty minutes sipping my wine and watching Champions League on the flat screen behind the bar. The woman worked furiously with her fingers, pausing only slightly to take a sip of wine or the bite out of a dumpling. I could see her expanding images, highlighting areas, and then referencing them to previous photos and files she had already saved.

"It's too simple." She finally said.

"What is?"

"All of it. The KGC were supposed to be masters at hiding their treasure if it is actually KGC clues we're following then why are we going through them so quickly?"

"Maybe that's just it. These clues are made to look like the KGC but in fact were planted by amateurs."

"That's a possibility. If someone like the Trenholms did steal the remains of the Confederate Treasury on their own, and without KGC approval, then they could have used a similar system to hide it."

"Makes sense to me."

Hannah looked at her screen for a moment. She was going between the photos she took at the wharf and at the school.

"There is a similar connection here between the pier, school, and even 1 Broad. In all the carvings, a ghost figure can be found at every location. However, at 1 Broad Street, there was a ship, which tells me it was pointing to the wharf. At the pier, I found an owl, which I believe was the locator for the school, however, with the school carvings I haven't found too much that really stands out."

"Nothing," I said. I had a mouth full of steam bun.

"The only thing is that instead of one ghost figure, like at the other markers, there are two. That's why I said these clues were too easy because I had already pinpointed a cemetery by aligning the cross with the map."

"So what's the problem?"

"Jack, don't get me wrong I love being right, but I'm afraid we've missed something important, and that's why it's been so easy. I'm starting to think that we are on a false trail."

"Then why are people shooting at us if we are following the wrong clues?"

"Good point. Maybe that's why they gave us warning shots instead of simply killing us." Hannah said.

"No, I think it's because they are afraid of the attention killing a visiting professor and a former FBI agent would bring. We are only dead if we actually find what they are hiding."

"That's reassuring," Hannah said, with a large gulp of wine to wash it down. "So, off to the cemetery tomorrow?"

"Sure, and hopefully it will be the last time either of us has to go to one in a long while."

CHAPTER 57

Life sometimes replicates film. Sometimes you associate something with a movie even though that picture never actually existed. Somewhere out there in a Hollywood vault is a scene and it begins with a gentle breeze along a coastal river, blades of grass blow as it moves across the marsh, and the Spanish moss is caught up in the passage of the wind pulling and tugging at the old branches of the oak it calls home. The camera pans out, and that one ancient oak tree becomes a hundred spaced across open land and speckled with magnolia trees in bloom. Moving down, the camera reveals that the exposed area is a cemetery adorned with family mausoleums, statues of angels and children, and hand carved stones. Dirt paths wind through the cemetery, and there, two people walk in a scene that is both haunting and reassuring to those that enter. As Hannah and I arrived at Magnolia Cemetery, I knew the scene, but I couldn't remember the ending to the movie.

"This way," Hannah said. She grabbed a map as we walked in.

We walked along the path, part dirt and part gravel, as it gently wove its way through the new section of the cemetery and into the old. Entering the original part of the graveyard brought with it a sense of importance. Here the trees grew thicker, their limbs stretched out longer, and the shadows cast made the area feel a bit haunted. The family plots were adorned with large mausoleums, Greek-inspired statues, and extravagantly carved headstones. One was even topped with a giant squid. The Trenholm plot was not what I expected as we approached. Instead of competing with the neighbors, the Trenholms were marked with a simple stone and each individual with smaller headstones.

"I was expecting something a little more ostentatious," I said.

"Maybe the plot was started before George A. Trenholm made all of his money, or maybe he didn't think his life had been statement enough."

We began to search the area for markings, but the Trenholm stones were small and lacking decoration, except for a name and dates. After about ten minutes of nothing, I sat down in the grass, feeling the warm sun on my face and the breeze coming up the hill from the water. It was quiet, and the only sound came from branches rattling and birds feeding down by the marsh. I scanned around me from where I sat and could see a monument dedicated to those lost during the Civil War. It had recently been ornamented with flags representing both the North and South in commemoration of the 150th Anniversary.

"What about that?" I said to Hannah and pointed at the monument.

"Seems obvious, but okay. I've got nothing to go on here."

Passing underneath the canopy of oak branches we moved towards the monument. Hannah stopped suddenly, and her mouth opened slightly.

"What is it?"

"I don't believe it." She said.

I finally locked onto what it was she had seen. On a magnolia tree, sheltered between two large oaks, were carvings. Not the carvings of a teenager's graffiti, but the familiar markings of the KGC. There was something different about these, and Hannah had realized it the moment her eyes caught sight of the magnolia tree. In the middle, the very center of the cluster of carvings was a pyramid topped with an all-seeing eye, and in the center of that eye was a hooked x.

Hannah had been quick to take pictures before, but this time she only stood and stared for a few moments.

"I see a lot of the same carvings as the other spots, mostly ones that are nonsense…at least I hope. The major differences are there are no ghost outlines here, and of course that dominant pyramid. I'm not sure how much it would have stood out to the casual observer, but I know for sure that wasn't on anything else we've seen." Hannah said, finally pulling out her phone. She began to take pictures but kept talking. "There also doesn't appear to be any numbers or dots that could represent a distance. I'm honestly not picking up any indicators of what or where these markings point to."

Hannah was hunched over taking shots closer to the base of the tree. In the back pocket of her jeans, she had stuck the information pamphlet on the cemetery. Four pictures graced the side of the brochure that I could see. One was a shot of the Civil War monument, another was the main cemetery building, and the third was that of a large mausoleum. The fourth picture was what had caught my eye. It was of another mausoleum, but it was shaped like a pyramid.

"I think I know where we need to go," I said to Hannah.

"How?"

"By staring at your ass."

Hannah looked as if she was going to slap the sarcasm right out of me, but then she realized what I had meant and pulled the pamphlet from her pocket. A smile appeared on her face as she checked the interior map for the crypt's location.

"Let's go." She said. "We might have gotten lucky again."

CHAPTER 58

A giant stone pyramid stood crowded among effigies, headstones, and palmetto trees. Two large marble stairs flanked with ornately carved urns led to the main entrance. The entrance itself was guarded on each side by a pair of swords carved from stone, and a copper door, green from the years, stood locked before us. The door, however, was not solid and was designed to allow light to pass entirely through the pyramid from the stained glass window on the opposite side. When I approached, the light shown through bright and a bountiful array of color came descending towards me. I realized that the copper doors were more like gates, allowing visitors to see the contents of the mausoleum without disturbing its residents. Straining myself to look inside, I could see that each wall was lined with three lavishly designed sarcophaguses, but it was the stained glass window and its vibrant light that drew my eye…because it too had an eye staring right back at me.

I left Hannah at the front of the pyramid and went to the backside to get a better view of the window. When I did the silence and tranquility of the cemetery was suddenly broken by the sound of a motor. Over my shoulder, from where we had just come, a truck came down the path filled with lawn care equipment. Ignoring the grounds crew, I took a page from Hannah's book and began taking pictures of the backside of the pyramid. It was very ordinary compared to the front, except for the window. The stained glass was in a triangle shape and designed in the image of the sun rising over the land, with the sun being the all-seeing eye. It was the same eye that graces the American dollar and conspiracy theorists loved. Within the stained glass window, the words *Rhymed Intro* were scrolled into the top above the all-seeing eye, and along the bottom *Carolina*. I couldn't wait to hear Hannah's opinion.

After a dozen or so shots with my phone's camera, covering every angle I thought Hannah might need, I headed back around to the other side. Instead of peering inside the tomb, I found Hannah kneeling before the urns at the front of the stairs. Her head turned from one to the other and then back again.

"What is it?" I asked, approaching.

"The urns hide the clues. There are markings like we've seen before on each of them, but they are mixed in with the artistic designs carved from the stone. It's genius because approaching the pyramid it would simply look like the work of a very talented stone carver, but up close there is more to it. Also, I found the hooked x." She pointed towards the door.

"Where?"

"The sword on the right-hand side of the door has a hooked x carved into its hilt."

"Nothing on the left?"

"Nothing, only the right one."

I thought for a moment. "Maybe that means we are only supposed to use the clues on the right urn then."

"That's actually a good thought." Hannah began taking pictures of the urn on the right-hand side of the stairs. Within a few short minutes, she had her shots. "In case your theory is wrong though…." Hannah trailed off as she began snapping pictures of the left one as well.

I moved behind where she was taking photos and started to slowly walk backward staring at the mausoleum. With the phone in hand, I attempted to get a shot of the whole scene, part for its beauty and partly because we may have missed something in the bigger picture. Snapping once then twice, I began to zoom in on an object towards the top on the capstone. It was something I hadn't seen from up close and now was struggling to see with the cheap image adjustments of my phone. Pulling the phone down from my line of sight I suddenly felt dizzy, and the pyramid began to sway in front of me. My knees buckled, and I went down.

CHAPTER 59

When I awoke, I was still lying on the ground in front of the pyramid. My view was foggy, and I could still feel that I clutched my phone in my hand. Sitting up, I realized that Hannah was gone, and so was the urn from the right side of the pyramid. The sound of an engine awakening made me turn to see a truck full of lawn equipment hurriedly driving towards the entrance of the cemetery.

"Hannah!" I yelled, to no response. "Hannah!" No response again.

Between the dust from the drive and my cloudy vision I couldn't make out the plates on the old rusted truck, but it was white, so I had something to go on. How many old, rusty, and white pickups could there be in the Lowcountry...probably more than I could count?

I was up, and my feet began to move quickly towards the front of the cemetery to where we had left the rental car. My head was now throbbing, so I knew that I had taken a hit from someone. We had walked so far through the cemetery that it took me a good five minutes to run back to the car at a full sprint. By the time I had gotten there the dust from the speeding truck had settled and it was long out of sight. Once in the car, I headed back towards downtown and got stuck in the cruise ship traffic that lined East Bay Street. While I waited in the stop and go jam of tourists, I called Colin, my former partner at the FBI, to tell him about Hannah being taken. He would have the connections and sway that I no longer did, and any help from the Bureau would get Hannah back faster.

My call with Colin was short and to the point. He needed to get moving quickly, and I could update him with all the little details later. It took me ten minutes in traffic to drive the half-mile from the Calhoun Street intersection to Market, where the cruise ships docked, and then traffic began to move a little better. I ignored my usual turn onto Church Street and instead headed one block further up Broad to Meeting. I took an aggressive pissed off left and made a beeline for George Trenholm's mansion.

The drive was of course gated, and the front parking was designated for horse carriage tours only, so I was forced to go down by White Point Gardens and walk back to the house. I rang the buzzer at the gate impatiently and finally simply held it down until someone answered.

"May I help you?" The voice of Trenholm's butler asked.

"I'm here to see Mr. Trenholm. It's Jack Francis." Like he didn't already know.

"Mr. Trenholm is not in at the moment."

"Tell him to get in touch with me...Immediately!" I screamed into the call box.

Trudging off like a scorned child, I returned to my rental car and drove back to the carriage house. What was I supposed to do? I had no idea who took Hannah, even though I assumed

Trenholm and his cronies were involved, but I had no way to find her. Something was there. Someway or some explanation that could lead me to her, but I needed to calm down and think. Getting back to my place, I poured four fingers of bourbon into a glass and called Colin back. Telling him the details, hearing them out loud, the whole story all at once might help me realize something I missed. Something maybe both of us missed, or maybe someone.

CHAPTER 60

After talking to Colin, he put me in touch with Special Agent Chris Meadows at the Bureau's office in Columbia. It wasn't the FBI's jurisdiction yet, put they could exert a little pressure on the local cops to get an APB out on the pickup. Charleston PD wouldn't have bothered with it until Hannah was missing for forty-eight hours if it weren't for the Bureau's insistance. I hadn't actually seen anyone take her, so instead of kidnapping the local boys would have labeled it a missing person. It was good to have friends in high places when you needed a little backup.

I drank enough bourbon to calm my nerves and help me fall asleep without waking up with a hangover. It was a particular skill I had developed over the years, and was thankful for the early start it allowed me on mornings when shit needed to get done.

Colin had insisted on flying down, so I was off to the airport to pick him up...along with his badge and gun. Finishing my coffee, I strapped my Glock inside my jacket and headed for the door. When I got downstairs and to the driveway, I could see that someone was waiting for me. Tommy Makem was sitting on Mrs. Legare's front porch having coffee with the woman.

"Tommy," I said cheerfully. It was for Mrs. Legare's benefit and not his. "What are you up to this morning?"

"Like I was telling your lovely landlord here, I came over to check on an old Cleveland pal."

"Great. Why don't you put your coffee down and jump in the car with me? I'm picking up a friend flying in from Ohio."

Tommy said a polite goodbye to Mrs. Legare, and I smiled and waved to her before getting in my rental car.

"What the hell are you doing here?" I asked Makem, as we backed out of the drive and pulled onto Church St.

"Came to talk. I heard about Hannah."

"Trenholm send you?"

"Actually, he did." He could see the anger rising in my face. "We're not part of this Jack. I'm not. Trenholm's not, or any of his associates."

"I'm not in a position to believe you. Especially, after being shot at and given a warning by you."

"That's understandable, and that's why I'm here. Trenholm figured there would be no talking to you without it turning into a shouting match, so he sent me. He felt our ties would help things along."

"So talk, and tell me why I should believe you." I stared straight ahead as we moved north towards the airport on Interstate 26.

"We've known about you and Hannah snooping around for a while, but you two weren't the only ones. From the very beginning, Trenholm understood that the death of his son, and the woman in the park, meant that someone with old ties was after him. He knew, and so did others in the neighborhood, what those killings signified. The connection was too obvious for him not to ignore."

I played dumb for a moment. "What connection?"

"Both victims, his son and the woman, were descendants of the owners of the Fraser, Trenholm, & Company. More exactly George A. Trenholm and Charles Fraser. Those two men had control of the business during the Civil War, a time when there were a lot of personal vendettas played out with the backdrop of the war."

"What you're telling me is that someone held onto a personal vendetta for a hundred and fifty years?"

"It's not so hard to fathom. Europeans hold onto to grudges longer than that."

Makem had a point. I knew of Irish families that came to America still holding onto feuds from the old country. I also was aware that he was talking about Elliott Tidwell. A man I had already met, and someone I had completely forgotten about. After he ran away, sword in hand, from my place I had put him far in the back of my mind.

"Let's say I believe you, then what?" I asked.

"Then I point you in the right direction, and you go get your girlfriend back."

I smirked at the girlfriend crack. "You know then where she is?"

"Not exactly, but I know who took her, what direction they headed, and where they could possibly be going in that direction."

"You were following Hannah and me at the cemetery. Weren't you?"

"I was there, but too far off to stop anything from happening…Scout's honor."

"You must have taken the urn then while I was out cold. Trenholm and his cronies probably would have wanted that as far away as possibly from me."

"What urn?" Makem asked.

"The one off of the pyramid mausoleum." The man looked clueless. "If you didn't take it then whoever kidnapped Hannah has it."

"What's so special about the urn?"

"Nothing," I said pulling up to the arrival area of the airport.

There was no sign of Colin yet, and I needed to circle around again before security crawled up my ass.

"I need to get out," Makem said.

I allowed him the opportunity before pulling away from the curb and joining the rest of the traffic doing laps around the airport and through the arrival area. From my mirror, I could see Makem put his phone to his ear. It took me three times around before I spotted Colin coming from the terminal, but I had already passed by him. On my fourth lap, I stopped. Colin tossed his bag into the trunk and got into the front seat. As soon as he closed the door, the rear passenger side door opened, and Makem got back in.

"Who's this?" Colin asked me.

I looked back at Makem with a question on my face.

"Drive," Makem said. "I'm going with you."

CHAPTER 61

Colin's broad shoulders were rigid as he sat is his stiff suit. He was a Bureau boy through and through, with every hair in place on his thick head, clean shaven, and each item of the clothing he wore was pressed, lint free and the perfect distance between cheap and expensive. By the way he was sitting, I could tell he was carrying, but he always did. Makem was too, and from the moment I introduced them I knew they were destined to hate each other.

"Why the sudden change of heart?" I asked Makem.

"I think you know."

"All I know is that you weren't informed on the urn. I tell you about it, and you make a phone call. Suddenly, you're back in the car with me. Want to explain?"

"Nope, I'm here to make sure you find your friend. Trenholm and I don't want you to point fingers at us for this one."

"Okay then," Colin interjected. "Tell us where she is."

"Elliott Tidwell. His family ties run a long way in the area, and they've had it out for the Trenholms since the war. When I was following Jack, I spotted him snooping around on occasion. I know for a fact he owns the pickup that drove off from the cemetery, and his family still owns a spit of land south of town. It's about the only thing they've been able to hang on to."

"Why's that?" Colin asked.

"After the war, some families in the South were able to carry on and rebuild fortunes. These were usually the ones who had the ability to pay the freemen for their work, and they kept their plantations running through crops and new diversifications. Others, who were barely staying afloat before Emancipation, struggled. The Tidwells struggled and throughout the years sold off everything from property to furniture to survive. Now, everything they had is gone except for a small sliver of land that was once a 700-acre plantation."

"Thanks for the history lesson," Colin said.

"Yeah, but where do we go?" I asked.

"South on 17. It will take us about an hour to reach the plantations along the Combahee River. Tidwell's place is out there somewhere."

"Somewhere?"

"I've got directions from Trenholm. No address, just directions. He said it's going to be pretty isolated and probably unmarked."

"Sounds fun. Three Ohio boys traipsing around in a remote forest in the Deep South, looking for a kidnapper who seems to hold onto Civil War grudges and runs around with a sword." I shook my head in disbelief.

"How do you know he carries a sword?" Makem asked.

"I've met the man before." I decided to fill him in on the little escapade I had with Tidwell. There was no reason to give Makem information I didn't have to, but that part seemed harmless.

"So you knew he was out there, and yet you blamed Trenholm first," Makem said.

"I was pretty sure that someone willing to fire warning shots at me would have no qualms about kidnapping."

We had sat quietly in the car for about half an hour before I pulled over to get gas. Colin got out and grabbed a chicken biscuit from a nearby restaurant as I pumped, and Makem got on his phone again. Another twenty minutes of driving and we turned right onto White Hall Road, and suddenly I felt transported back in time. Life here seemed untouched, quiet, and in a confusing way how it was supposed to be. The small winding road, stone walls, the colonial church, and ancient trees had me relaxed as I drove. But the further we got off of the highway my apprehension grew as we became more surrounded by the isolation.

CHAPTER 62

"Stop the car," Makem said. "Pull over to the side here."

I pulled the car to the edge of the gravel and got out to take a look at my surroundings. Colin squeezed his large frame as he struggled to get out from between the car door and a rusted barbed wire fence on the edge of the woods.

"Thanks," Colin said to me, finally getting free. "Where are we?"

"The Combahee River Basin," Makem said. "Once home to the largest rice plantations in the country."

"Why is it so quiet?" Colin asked.

"Because there is literally nothing around us. We are probably a good mile away from the next plantation and another mile up the drive to get to the house." Makem pulled his gun, a 38, checked it and then holstered it back under his jacket. Next, he pulled his phone. "No signal. We're on our own boys. Oh, and don't get hurt. The next closest hospital you'd be willing to go to is back in Charleston."

"That's comforting," I said. "Where to now?"

All I could see around me was woods. Two dirt paths led into the trees on both sides of the road, but nothing else.

"These are hunting trails. Most of the plantations around here are now used as game retreats. Trenholm told me to take this one, and it will connect with the Tidwell property in about half a mile."

"Are you sure?" Colin asked.

"Almost positive, but no promises. I've never been this far out before."

"How do we know the Tidwell property?" I asked.

"I was told this trail should take us out of the woods right behind the old slave cabins on the property. From there, we're on our own."

Makem began to lead the way as we took the trail on the far side of the road. I looked at Colin, he looked at me, and both of us rechecked our Glocks.

We walked briskly but quieted. The only sounds came from the occasional bird and the rustle of leaves. The woods were a mix of pine, oak, and palmetto fronds mixed with a tangle of vines and low-lying wet areas. At one point the trail crossed a creek, and I could see the marsh it flowed into from a distance. It was a weird contrast of environments. I was deep in the woods, but I knew within minutes I could be at the marsh, then a creek, then a river, and finally out to sea.

It took us about twenty minutes of walking in silence before Makem held up, and Colin and I gathered with him at the edge of the woods. About ten yards away were a cluster of run-down shacks, which I had to assume were the old slave cabins. I could also see a fence in a state of disrepair and across a stretch of grass a drive, not much wider than the hunting trail, which cut an open field in half.

"The house is that way." Makem pointed to our left.

"Are you sure?" Colin asked.

"I'm confident, and there is supposed to be a barn on the property too."

"We need to split up," Colin said.

"I'll walk the tree line to the right and get on the other side of that field," I said. "Why don't the two of you work your way left and split up when you get closer to the house." I didn't trust Makem and was sure Colin hated him, so I figured they could keep a good eye on each other. "When we get up there, one of you go to the house, and the other find that barn. I'll head to the house as well."

"I'll take the home too," Makem said. "Let's meet around back and formulate a plan before heading inside."

"Since you two are taking the house, why don't I go on my own on the other side of the field?" Colin asked.

"No. I need you to stick with Makem on this side of the property. The slave cabins are on this side of the drive, and I know the river is too, which means I have to assume the barn was built over here as well. You wouldn't want your storehouse too far from your workers or your loading area. If I'm right then, that means we need two people to stay on this side so they can split up."

"Makes sense," Colin said.

"All right, let's go find Hannah," I said, moving off alone through the woods to my left.

I watched as the two of them moved left. Slowly walking through the trees making as little sound as possible. When I finally made it to the edge of the drive, I crouched down for a moment and sat perfectly still, quietly listening. There wasn't a sound but Mother Nature. I glanced up the drive to my left and again to my right before darting across the dirt drive as fast as I could. Slipping back among the trees, I crouched once again a listened. The sound came from a distance and was growing. I could hear an engine and rubber on well-packed dirt. The motor seemed a little rough as it grew closer, and then I began catching glimpses of white between the tree branches. Coming up the drive and heading towards the house was the same white pickup truck that I had seen at the cemetery. It now lacked the lawn equipment, but it sure carried the wirehaired silhouette of Elliott Tidwell.

CHAPTER 63

Knowing where your enemy is helps...a lot. I now had an idea where Tidwell was, and it allowed me to move faster through the woods and towards the old plantation house. The noise from his truck would cover up the sound of me crashing through the trees, and the trees would keep me hidden from view. The best thing we had going for us was the fact that Tidwell's truck was old and loud, which would warn Colin and Makem that he was coming, and notify me when he passed my location and moved further down the drive. The engine turning off would be my warning to tighten up and go on the defensive again. My hope was that Colin and Makem were ahead of me and saw Tidwell get out. That way we would have a grasp on his whereabouts, and maybe he would lead one of them to Hannah.

I was in sight of the dilapidated home as the truck motor was turned off, but I could not see Tidwell or his pickup. Stopping in my current position, I squatted among some palms and watched the front of the house. For about five minutes, I sat and waited, and when no one appeared I assumed Tidwell had gone in a back way. Making my way slowly and calmly to the edge of the clearing that surrounded the old plantation home, I could finally get a visual on the barn and a glimpse of water that ran past the property. I didn't know if it was the Combahee River or some tidal creek and really it didn't matter. The point was I finally was getting a grasp of the layout, and that was important. Now, somehow, I had to make my way from the edge of the woods and to the house without being seen.

Towards the back of the home, there was a cluster of trees dominated by an ancient oak. Its branches spread wide like an octopus encompassing most of the yard. Around its outstretched arms were clusters of unkempt shrubs, flowering hydrangeas, and crape myrtle. If I could make it there, I would have a perfect view of the house and be hidden, but between me and the old oak was nothing, nothing but a stretch of open grass and weeds. I would simply have to make a run for it, too risky and unprofessional, but it was my only shot.

Sprinting as lightly as I could, I waited for the sound of a door, a raving madman with a sword, or more simply a gunshot but there was nothing. I made it to a spot where a large oak branch with the circumference of a truck tire mingled with a cluster of shrubs. I knelt, catching my breath, and began to scan the back of the house for any activity. There was none. I could hear an outboard motor in the distance as it planed the calm waters of the river. It distracted me, and I wished I was onboard heading out on a fishing trip. A tap on my shoulder and I was scared back into reality.

"Makem, you scared the shit out of me."

"I know." The man whispered with a smile. "I was on the other side of the tree when I saw you sprinting across the lawn like an ostrich with its head cut off."

"It wasn't my best moment, but it was my only play."

"Figured. Colin's checking out the barn, and from what I've seen Tidwell's inside the house. He pulled up in that old truck and went in the back entrance with a bag of groceries."

"Any movement from inside?"

"Nothing."

"I counted three entrances to the house. Coincidence?"

"More like dumb luck," Makem said. "So the plan is to wait for Colin and all go in together?"

"From what I see there is the main entrance in the front and out back here there is a door that parallels that. There is also the smaller opening that probably once was the servants' door below the porch. I would hate for the two of us to go in guns blazing and Tidwell escape through the third. I have to assume he knows these woods like the back of his hand."

"Can't agree more. So, we sit and wait?"

"For now."

CHAPTER 64

The man peered out the window towards the back of the property. He had a cup of fresh coffee in his hand and a sword strapped to his hip. Tidwell wasn't sure that he had seen anything at all, but something had caught his attention. A blur out of the corner of his eye had seemed to dash behind a cluster of bushes around the great oak at the back of his family's property. It could have been nothing, it could have been simply an animal, or it could have been something else. He sipped and watched, waiting for more movement. If something or someone were behind those bushes, they would move sooner or later.

Tidwell stood in the old dining room of the house. Wood floorboards squeaked and needed to be replaced. The table was missing, being sold off years ago along with paintings and a buffet that had graced the room, and once where there had been expensive curtains now hung three dollar blinds from the local hardware store. If there was a better representation of the disgrace, his family suffered Tidwell couldn't think of it. Keeping an eye on the window, Tidwell made his way over to the only piece of furniture left in the room. It was a wooden cabinet that stood seven feet tall and had two doors filled with elaborate carvings. Perfectly dust free, the cabinet was where generations of Tidwells had stored the family guns. A southerner would sell off land and possessions to keep the family home, but the guns were always the last to go. The Tidwells had never been desperate enough to part ways with their small arsenal.

Every item in the cabinet was as sparkling and spotless as the sword at Tidwell's side. Each piece was polished, barrels cleaned, and all loaded. Grabbing two double barrel pinfire pocket pistols, Tidwell stuck them in his belt and then retrieved a more modern Winchester 1873 model rifle. It was one of the last items in the cabinet that the family had been able to afford.

With his eyes staying steady on the bush line in the back of the house, Tidwell stood the rifle up by the window and returned to his coffee, sipping, waiting, and watching for the slightest of movement. If the leaves even rustled, he would probably shoot. At best, it would be a Trenholm or even Jack Francis, and at worst it would be a rabbit or some dumbass who accidently stumbled onto the property. Ever year a couple northerners would rent a nearby plantation for a hunting trip and every year a few would get lost in the woods. Maybe if Tidwell shot a few, they would be more careful about where they wandered off to.

Impatience grew with every minute and after about five Tidwell was about to give up. He had things to do and possibly, just possibly, he could be on alert for nothing. Picking up the rifle, he was about to give up when he caught a glimpse of a man moving around the edge of the barn off to the left of where he was looking. At first, the man had been simply a blur in the corner of his eye, but he appeared again moving towards the front of the house. Tidwell didn't recognize him but was worried because he had the appearance of a government agent. This was not one of Trenholm's people or Jack Francis. In fact, quite the opposite of what Tidwell had expected. The broad shoulders, polished suit, and hair combed and locked into place suggested more. Maybe taking the woman had brought the wrong kind of attention, and he still hadn't had the chance to get any information from her.

Watching the man with one eye, Tidwell scanned for others. No one would be dumb enough to come out here alone, and if this man was a government agent wouldn't he have a partner? That blur he saw earlier. The thought that someone was in the bushes behind the house. That had to be where the other was hiding. Not wanting to make the first move, Tidwell waited. He knew he had to get out of the mess taking the woman had made, but Tidwell also knew his retribution would not end without a fight. If he had to, he would kill them all. No one was around for miles, and the sound of gunfire in these woods came from hunters all the time. And getting rid of a few bodies, well, that was simply too easy. Or better yet he might make a display of them to prove to Francis and Trenholm that he meant business.

CHAPTER 65

Giving Colin a chance to make his way around to the front of the house, Makem and I began our plan of attack. There were two possible points of entry for us, so we split up. Makem took the entrance on the main floor opposite of where Colin would come in on the front of the house, while I was going to go in the servants' entry. We moved quickly from our spot behind the bushes and broke off when we reached the house. I went under the porch and Makem up the stairs to the main level. There were two ways of going in; loud and fast or quiet and slow. As a group, we decided that quiet and slow was our best bet.

The servants' entrance had a door that was misshapen due to the warping of wood over the years. With gun in hand, I pulled it open very gently waiting for the rusty hinges to make a sound. They didn't. There was a small entry room with storage shelves that led into the kitchen. Coffee was on the counter and appeared to be fresh from the smell wafting through the home. There was no movement and no sounds coming from anywhere. I couldn't hear footsteps on the floor above me and wondered if Colin and Makem had made it inside yet.

I looked over the kitchen while keeping an eye on the two doorways leaving the room. The first one, to the right of where I came in housed the stairwell, and the second continued on to a storage area. Remembering back to Hannah and my visit to Ashley Hall, I had to assume that this area once housed furniture that the slaves could change out with the season. Now it was empty. The floor was dusty, and there was a table, laundry sink, and some fishing equipment in the corner. If the room was used, it was not often.

Moving on I began to realize that the first floor of the house was primarily a basement, only not underground like in the North. The second floor above me was the central area of the home, with the third containing the bedrooms. It was similar to what I had seen at the McBee House at Ashley Hall, but not on the same scale in size or grandeur. I cleared three more rooms that I had to assume had once been used as storage before heading back towards the stairs. There was still no noise coming from above me and I began to get a little worried.

The stairs leading up to the main floor were dirty, but it was also obvious that they had been used recently and often. The dust and dirt had collected to the outer edges of the wooden steps from the breeze caused by someone walking up and down them. Moving slowly, each time the weight of my foot touched the wood it gave a small groan. The sound wasn't much, but in the deathly silence of the house, it seemed like a thunderous roar announcing my arrival. There wasn't a thing I could do and continued step by step.

The stairwell opened up into the main hall of the house from the entrance point hidden behind the central staircase. With my gun out in front, I moved into the open room checking the first doorway I came to…nothing. The second, third, and fourth rooms were all empty too. And I mean empty. There was little furniture in the house, and most rooms had none at all. I saw a cabinet in one room and a lawn chair and small television in another, but that was it. My gut had a feeling I didn't like, and I was beginning to wonder where everybody was. Four other people should have been in the house. I knew for sure Colin and Makem, but I had to assume Hannah and Tidwell were here somewhere too.

When I took my first step to begin the climb up to the next floor, I finally heard something. It was the sounds of whispering. Too soft to hear the words or even who it was, but I could tell that upstairs someone was talking. With a little bit of excitement and apprehension, I began to make the ascent. At the top of the landing, the floor was broken up with two rooms on either side. The noise came from the door on the far side and to my right. Quietly, I moved with my back to the wall taking silent miniature steps. The voices had stopped, but I knew whoever was in the room still had to be there. Reaching the doorway, I stopped and listened again, but there was nothing. In one quick movement, I made the turn into the room with my Glock at the ready, but it wouldn't be needed. Inside was a barren room and dirty floor that housed a small cot. Colin was kneeling by the bed, gun aimed at me and the doorway. Behind him, and still half tied, was Hannah looking more pissed than scared.

CHAPTER 66

Helping Colin, we quickly finished untying Hannah, and the three of us moved towards the door. She gave me a quick squeeze of the hand as we got up. It might have been a thank you or simply a sign that she was okay, but either way, it was nice.

"Where's Makem?" I asked Colin.

"No idea. He took the main floor, and I came up here. I guess you didn't pass him on the way up."

"I haven't seen anyone," I said in a whisper.

As a group, the three of us moved out into the hallway and towards the stairs. Colin had taken the lead, and I was in the back with Hannah in between us. At the top of the stairs, Hannah paused suddenly.

"I've found Makem." She said.

Through the window at the rear of the house, we could see Makem moving awkwardly towards the river. With his gun in one hand, he struggled to carry a massive urn-shaped object in the other. He walked like a penguin as he balanced the urn on the side of his hip for support.

"That's why he wanted to come," I said.

"What's he carrying?" Colin asked.

"I'll explain later, but for now let's go catch him."

Our group changed gears and speed up as we made our way down the stairs to the main floor of the house. We took the back door out to the porch and down another flight of stairs to the overgrown grass below. Makem was still within site, but in the distance I could hear the drumming of an outboard motor revving at high speed.

We ran, but even in his challenging state Makem was closing in on the old dock. I wondered for a second if the rotted wood could even hold the large man and the hefty urn, but I never got a chance to find out. Within five feet of the water's edge, a man jumped from the woods in front of Makem and swung the butt end of a rifle across the side of his head. With a thud and a cloud of dirt billowing around him, Makem went down hard dropping the urn and his gun. Elliott Tidwell kicked the gun away from the fallen Makem and then glared at our group still fifty yards away. With a wicked smile, he grabbed the urn from where it had fallen and darted into the woods as fast as he had appeared. Tidwell was a scrawny man, but he made off with the urn more swiftly than any of us had expected.

Hannah was the first to get her run into another gear as she surged ahead of Colin and I. We took her lead and soon found ourselves in an all-out sprint for the woods where Tidwell had disappeared. He couldn't get far carrying that urn, and there were three of us and only one of him…odds were in our favor I thought.

The three of us hit the woods with a crash with no thought of stopping to check on Makem. He had obviously come here for the urn only, so nobody was feeling sorry for him at the moment. I also could hear the boat approaching and figured whoever was picking him up could see to the Irishman's wounds.

Beneath the cover of the trees, there was no sign of Tidwell. The three of us spread out. Hannah was in the middle, Colin was to her left, and I was on the right, as we navigated the terrain. We followed the sound of Tidwell ahead of us barely audible over our own noise. It seemed that he was moving at the same speed as us, but that couldn't be possible. Hannah stopped so quickly that Colin and I had run past her before either noticed. There was silence in the woods. The noise from our running was gone, and so was the sound of Tidwell.

The three of us walked a little closer together with heads turning looking, waiting and watching for something to move. No birds chirp. No leaves crunched underfoot, and the breeze seemed to have even paused momentarily.

"What happened?" Hannah asked.

"He is armed. Maybe he realized running was pointless and he is hunkering down behind some log waiting for us." I said.

"I wouldn't," Colin interjected. "That rifle he hit Makem with was an old Winchester, and the only other thing I saw on him was two pistols in his waistline. They actually looked like dueling pistols."

"He has a thing for antique weapons. I know for a fact he carries a sword too."

"I didn't see it on him," Hannah said to me.

The silence was broken as the firing of a gun echoed between the trees. Birds silent and in hiding suddenly flew off from the trees and bushes around us. Instinctively, I looked towards the area where the noise had come, and then with a gaping mouth back towards Colin and Hannah. Colin looked back at me and dropped to the ground for cover. Hannah was already down, and I followed suit just as another shot came from the woods in front of us.

"How many shots do you think he has with that rifle?" I yelled to Colin, not realizing the woods had grown silent again.

"Who knows? I didn't see any kind of ammo belt on him. We need to make our way closer. I don't hear any movement, so he must have himself pinned in somewhere."

I looked over at Hannah, and she looked towards me with a forced grin. Then the three of us began to crawl our way through the South Carolina woods towards the spot where the shots had come from.

CHAPTER 67

Like crawling through a fox hole, I took the lead and slithered my way across sharp palms, fire ants, roaches, and mud. Colin was behind me, and Hannah had fallen to the rear. Tidwell had to know we were on the move from the rustling of our movements, but he stayed quiet. His silence told me that he either did not have a sight of us or he had limited ammunition. In a perfect world, it would be both.

A hundred feet or so of crawling through the muddy forest floor and I finally could make out a spot where Tidwell was probably hiding. A little shack, at one time painted white, had been taken over by Mother Nature. A small window faced us framed in Kudzu and darkened on the inside. I looked at Colin, and without a word he began to move off to the left to get around the shack. I looked for Hannah when Colin moved, and I couldn't see her. With a strain, I looked over my right shoulder hoping she had moved to my side, but she wasn't there. I sat up slightly and turned myself around so I could clearly see the woods behind me and there was no sign of Hannah anywhere. How did she just disappear?

My movement must have set an alarm off for Tidwell because another shot rang out and clipped by me and buried itself into a tree trunk. I turned back onto my stomach and got low with the ground. There was no way I could go find Hannah without dealing with Tidwell first. Now that he had my location I couldn't go lolly-gagging through the woods trying to find her.

Sliding my Glock back out I decided to give Tidwell some of his own medicines and fired a couple rounds into the darkened window of the cabin. Maybe I would get lucky and hit him, but at least I would let him know what it felt like to be shot at. After my shots, I waited in silence before moving closer towards the shack. Wanting to stay out of view I had to be careful, but I also needed a better angle to see into the window. Colin was out there somewhere and hopefully he was getting closer from my distraction of Tidwell. When I got the angle I wanted, I stopped my crawl and positioned myself to take another shot. The window was still dark from the inside, but at least now I had a larger target to fire into.

I put another shot through the center of the window and then tried two through the rotted planks on either side of it. Tidwell had to be tucked in there somewhere, and even though I didn't really want him dead, I wouldn't have minded wounding the crazy man. For the next five minutes, I took sporadic shots towards the ramshackle building wanting to keep Tidwell's attention on me. The darkened window lit up with light and in that second three shots fired. Two from a Glock and the third from another weapon.

Slowly, I got up from my position and when no one tried to shoot my head off I ran towards the building and around to the back side. When I reached the doorway, Colin was leaning against the frame breathing heavily. The heavy breathing worried me, and I thought he had been hit, but the FBI Agent shook my worries of with a wave.

"He shot the minute he realized the door behind him was opening," Colin said regaining his breath. "Luckily, I had gone small, and he fired where I would have been standing."

I poked my head inside the shack. There was blood pooling below the window. Old bottles filled a corner, dusty and surrounding a small still. Tidwell lay towards the opposite end with his head against the wall and feet displayed out towards the center of the structure. He had taken two shots to the chest, and I also noticed one in the shoulder. I must have wounded him at some point. On the floor rolling next to Tidwell, was the urn going back and forth slowly until it came to rest just past his outstretched hand.

"Where's Hannah?" I heard Colin ask.

CHAPTER 68

At the realization that I had forgotten about Hannah, Colin and I quickly left the lifeless Tidwell and sprinted back into the woods towards the direction we had come. There was no silent stalking this time. Instead, there was crashing and yelling from two grown men as we called out for Hannah and moved with a disregard for bushes and branches in our way.

"Son of a bitch!" I heard Colin yell, as a branch came back to smack him in the back of his head.

It was then that I noticed Hannah, laying only a few yards from where I had last seen her. She was facing down in the dirt, one arm outstretched, and the opposite leg pulled forward as if to crawl. Hannah lay motionless, but I could see her back move up and down with slow struggled breaths.

"Hannah!" I called out to her, moving quickly to her side.

She looked up at me for a moment and then reached towards her outstretched left leg with her hand. I could see now what I hadn't crawling in front of her. There was blood pooling around her upper thigh and being soaked up by the earth.

"Colin, over here." I waved desperately. "She's been hit."

Colin rushed over as I slowly flipped Hannah onto her side so I could tie my jacket around her thigh to provide pressure and a temporary bandage.

"I'll get the car and bring it as close to the edge of the woods as I can," Colin said. He stood and began to crash through the foliage as fast as his large frame could.

I wasn't a doctor, an EMT, or even had training beyond basic CPR so what I had done for Hannah so far was all I was going to be able to manage. Lifting Hannah, I carried her in my arms carefully back the way we had originally come. It was the only sure route I had to get out of this forest without taking the risk of getting lost or getting stuck in the marsh. Between the extra weight of carrying Hannah and navigating the obstacles around me, it took me way too long to reach the clearing. Colin pulled up with the car as I came out of the woods and hurried to help me get Hannah into the back seat. I jumped up front to drive, and Colin grabbed the passenger seat, and we were off tossing mud from the rear tires as I drove through the yard.

A glance from my rearview told me that Makem was no longer laying on the ground knocked out, but I did see a small center console at the dock. The thought was quick and then lost in the moment, but I wondered where they had gone off to. I didn't care. Hannah's bleeding was getting worse, and I was worried that the bullet hit something big. I knew that if the femoral artery had been severed by the shot, then Hannah was short on time.

We raced down the drive and back out the small winding roads that had led us to the plantation. Colin tried desperately to get a cell phone signal, but it wasn't working. We needed to have an ambulance meet us because I doubted Hannah would make it back into Charleston without medical attention. It had seemed like forever before we escaped the time warp of White Hall Lane and exploded back out onto Highway 17.

Within minutes, Colin had emergency services on the phone and used his FBI sway to bypass any hesitation the operator might have had with our request. From the back seat, Hannah lay silent, but I could still see her breathing and the blood stain on my coat getting bigger. Twenty minutes later, the ambulance met us at a barren spot of road along the Ashepoo River, and the EMTs went to work on Hannah. They had her in the back of the ambulance, and I jumped into ride along just as they began to stabilize her. With a quick wave to Colin, we were off moving again and heading back towards Charleston with lights and sirens screaming.

CHAPTER 69

The waiting room at the medical university in downtown Charleston was like any other I had been in, and I hated it. There is no place in the world worse than a hospital waiting room. It was nothing but a container for worried, emotional, and anxious people and today I was one of them. Hannah had been in surgery for a while, and I was getting uneasy. My legs were tapping, and I couldn't figure out if I wanted to sit down or pace. The vibration in the pocket of my pants was a welcome relief, as I stepped outside to answer.

"How is she?" Colin asked.

"Don't know yet. They're still in surgery."

"It'll be okay. She must have taken that first shot that came at us."

"I was thinking the same thing," I said. "How's it going on your end?"

I knew Colin would have to go back to the scene, report to his superiors and call everything into the local authorities. It was a red tape nightmare that I was glad I didn't have to deal with.

"The Agent in Charge out of the Columbia, SC field office is pissed at us, but he'll have our back when it comes to dealing with the locals. I've met some of the sheriff's deputies, and we are heading back to Tidwell's plantation now. I'll show them around and give them my report. Anything you want said, or even left out?"

"Let's try to keep why Tidwell took Hannah out of it for now," I said. "The locals can work on a motive if they really have the desire to know."

"Sounds like a good idea."

"Also, I noticed a small center console sitting at the dock when we pulled away. My guess is that the boat was Makem's ride out of there, so keep an eye out. I'm sure they're long gone by now, though."

"Will do. I'll call when I get a chance and update you a little more once I'm able to get a signal again." Colin was already beginning to cut out as he spoke.

"All right. And I'll leave a message if I find out any progress on Hannah."

With the cell phone back in my pocket, I returned to the depressing waiting room. Colin was going to have his hands full with the locals. They would be respectful of his FBI creds, but this was their turf, and I was sure they would be upset with what we had done. I also wondered what kind of influence Trenholm would have over their actions. If he wanted to press their investigation into our little escapade one way or another, I was sure he could. In that case, having the Bureau in Columbia behind us was important.

Trenholm's influence, I was sure stretched to the South Carolina capital, but I doubted he had infiltrated the Bureau there. The FBI wasn't made up of good ole' boys from the Lowcountry, so I highly doubted Trenholm would have much persuasion inside their Columbia location. At the same time, I could see Trenholm wanting the whole thing kept quiet. Getting us in trouble in order to have us out of the way was one thing, but I doubted he would want to bring attention to why we were there in the first place, or why Hannah had been kidnapped.

CHAPTER 70

I sat by Hannah's bed and watched her sleep for a few hours until the nurse convinced me that it was time to leave. She would sleep through the night, I was told, and I headed back to my place to freshen up and get some rest myself. The hospital was about a mile walk from my home on Church Street, so there was no reason I couldn't walk back. It would give me some time to clear my head, and figure out if this was how the game was going to end. Having lost a woman I was close to a few months ago, Hannah's brush with death today had me re-thinking life. I had left Cleveland and came south to think and take time for myself away from the lifestyle I had been leading. When Alex had been shot in Cleveland, it took a lot out of me. We might not have been anything more than lovers, but when someone dies because they were involved with you, it makes you re-evaluate the type of life you lead. Now, within a year, two women I got close to had been shot. Fortunately, Hannah would survive, but once again I found myself wanting to run.

When I got in the door, Colin was already there. I gave a puzzled look at him sitting on the couch watching TV, shoes off, feet up, and palming a cold beer.

"I convinced Mrs. Legare to let me in." He said.

"I didn't realize you knew her."

"Just met her when I got here, but an FBI badge and knowing your whole life story was enough to convince her that I was a friend."

"You're not getting a hotel?" I asked.

"Maybe, I wanted to check on you first. How's Hannah?"

"Out of surgery and sleeping like a baby. The doctor said she's going to be fine." I went to the fridge, grabbed a beer, and joined Colin on the couch. "How do I get myself into these situations?"

"Don't blame yourself," Colin said. "This isn't Alex all over again. That was a trained assassin, and she was a target. Hannah was merely in the wrong place at the wrong time."

"That's almost worse."

"But she'll be okay, and there is no reason to blame yourself."

"You're probably right, but it doesn't make me feel any better. At the Bureau or in the Army I was prepared to have those around me put in danger. It was our job and something we all signed up for, but Hannah's a college professor. Where did she sign up for this?"

"Hannah, like Alex, chose her own path. No, she did not want to get kidnapped or be shot at by a crazy Civil War reenactor, but continuing on the case and pushing it further with all the warning signs was her choice as much as yours."

"It's true, but it doesn't make me feel any better," I said, sipping my beer.

"So what now?"

"I'm not sure. We never proved who killed Jason or the other woman, but I'm pretty sure it was Tidwell. Now that he's dead it seems pointless to carry on down that road."

"What about your little treasure hunt? That seems to be where the trouble all started." Colin pointed out.

"Well, it was as much of a treasure hunt as it was a quest for answers. Tidwell believed his family had been somehow betrayed by the Trenholms, and therefore they had betrayed the South, but I'm starting to think he was wrong."

"What do you mean?"

"The first time I ran into Tidwell he gave us the impression that the Trenholms had betrayed the South by stealing the Confederate Treasury and using it to rebuild their fortune. The group charged with guarding the treasure was led by Tidwell's ancestor, and when it went missing he was blamed and the family name became ruined throughout the South. I'm beginning to believe Tidwell was right, his family was set up to take the fall, but I think the Trenholms had the backing of the KGC."

The KGC?" Colin asked.

"The Knights of the Golden Circle, the Southern secret society I told you about on the phone."

"Right. Let me get this straight. You think the KGC stole their own treasure and purposely put the blame on the Tidwells. I have to ask, why?"

"I'm not sure, but I get the feeling that Trenholm, Makem, and their cronies are the KGC. Which means that they are protecting the treasure. Tidwell wanted to find it to prove that the Trenholms stole it in the first place, but now I believe that's pointless because the rightful owners are still in possession."

"So that's why he wanted Hannah. For the letter and then the urn."

I looked at Colin for a moment and then it dawned on me. "The urn, where is it?"

CHAPTER 71

The next morning Hannah was awake and getting closer to being her old self. Before I even finished my first cup of coffee, my phone was ringing with a list of demands. The first thing Hannah wanted was out of the hospital, but that wasn't going to happen without the doctor's okay. Instead, I appeased her by bringing by a charger for her cell, her trusty tablet, and a comfy sweatshirt she liked to lay around in. Colin dropped me off at the medical college, and he headed back out to Tidwell's plantation to work the crime scene with the locals. He didn't have to be out there, but we needed to know if the urn was still where we had left it in the shack. I was also beginning to wonder where Tommy Makem had hidden himself away.

"Good morning, Sunshine. How are you feeling?" I said to Hannah, as I walked into her room.

"Good morning. I'm doing well. I think I've got most of my blood back" Her smile was as bright as the sun coming in through the window. "Did you find everything okay?"

"Yeap, I've got it all right here." I patted the canvas bag I had in my hand before delicately placing it on her lap. Her leg was still heavily bandaged, but besides that she looked amazingly better. "Have you had breakfast yet?"

"Some powdered eggs and toast." She answered.

I watched as she went through the bag and then struggled to put the sweatshirt on. A look that said *back off* came across Hannah's face as I moved in to help, so I settled into a chair and waited. Once the sweatshirt debacle was over, she plugged her phone into the wall and booted up her tablet. Apparently, Hannah wasn't wasting any time reconnecting with the world.

"What happened?" She asked.

"What do you mean?"

"Yesterday. The only thing I remember was getting shot. Everything else is a blur."

I hadn't really thought about that, so I filled her in on everything. Even the part about Colin and me losing the urn.

"It's not a huge deal if he doesn't find it," Hannah said calmly.

"Why?"

"The pictures. It's why I also have copies of all my research. See." She held up her tablet and scrolled through the pictures she took of the urn at the cemetery. "We probably have everything we need right here."

"Do we even want to bother? Tidwell is dead, and I'm pretty sure he killed Jason, so why move forward and risk anything or anyone else."

"Because, we don't know why Jason died. I know it's for a secret his family has kept since the Civil War, but what secret is worth the price of a life? That's what has kept me intrigued. I don't care about finding lost Confederate treasure. It will end up in a museum if I have my way. What I care about is the why."

"Always the good historian. We know what happened, but the real question is the why. Okay, I get it. Here's what I'm thinking. I think Tidwell was crazy as shit, and I don't believe the Trenholms actually stole anything," I said.

"What do you mean?"

"Trenholm and Makem are working together, and it seems they are only a small portion of a bigger group. It's the only way the local media and the South of Broad neighborhood haven't gone crazy over two killings…there is an influential group at play, which makes me believe the KGC is alive and well in Charleston."

"All right, I'm on the same page with you so far."

"Great, I was worried you would blow my theory right up."

"I still may," Hannah said.

"Anyways, go back to the end of the Civil War and Tidwell's great-great grandpappy, or whoever he was, is hauling the remains of the Confederate Treasury to a secluded spot to be loaded onto blockade runners, but when they arrive the treasure is missing. Tidwell believed that his ancestor was set up by Trenholm to take the blame, and I think he was, but not for the same reason."

"You're losing me."

"I think it was a giant illusion. The KGC and George A. Trenholm used the elder Tidwell and his men as a decoy for where the real money was going. Laying the blame on them for the theft would create even a larger distraction. The Union Army and later the Federal Government would take the rumors of Tidwell and his men stealing the remains of the Confederate Treasury as fact when they conducted a search for the gold. Meanwhile, the KGC, led by Trenholm had already moved and hidden the treasure to the actual location," I finished proudly.

"It does make sense."

"My question is, and this may prove my theory correct, how was the Trenholm family fortune rebuilt after the war? Did he suddenly have money, which would indicate he stole the gold, or did he build it up through connections and deals already established. Trenholm was in a position to take a huge fall when the war ended. As a smart business man, he must have been prepared for it. He could have easily had the means in place to reestablish his fortune knowing the US Government would punish him for his ties to the Confederacy."

"The answer is a little of both. Through my research with Jason, we found that the Trenholm family never became paupers. When Trenholm was released from Federal custody, he simply went back to the life he was used to. I'm sure part of it was an illusion or show for the public to keep up perception, but James Trenholm was continuing to run Fraser, Trenholm, & Company from Liverpool...out of reach of the Federal Government."

"So I'm right then?" I asked.

"Nothing positive, but your theory seems to hold."

"Then why keep looking? It seems we have all the answers." I said.

"Not all. Why would a group of men hold on for something this long? Why would they still protect it with their lives and to the threat of others? There's something else there, and I need to know."

CHAPTER 72

Hospitals are horrible places in my opinion, but sitting there all afternoon with Hannah wasn't bad. Colin called with the news that there was no sign of the urn, and we had to assume Makem had gotten a hold of it after we left. While this was bad news, it also provided us with a little more insight into our theory. From the moment we saw Makem heading towards the dock at the old plantation house with the urn, I knew it was the only reason he had come out there with us. The fact that he stuck around after being whacked in the head was a sign of its importance to him and his small group of friends. I also had to believe that they were relieved and felt a little bit more secure knowing that the urn was not in mine or Hannah's hands, but what they didn't know was that we had all the information we needed from the pictures on the tablet.

The KGC or whomever Trenholm and Makem represented would have to assume that they had stopped our little treasure hunt by taking possession of the urn. It would give us an opportunity to work without being followed. Looking at the still bandaged leg of Hannah, I was also acutely aware that I was on my own for the time being. None of that mattered at the moment, though. We had been over the pictures all afternoon with no luck in trying to decipher the message. I was getting antsy with every brick wall we hit, and deep down inside I had already concluded that it would be Hannah that solved this riddle and not me.

"I'm going to let you get some rest," I said. "We've been at it since breakfast, and you need some sleep."

"I'm fine. What we need is to figure this thing out."

"It's only been a day your body needs to rest and heal. I'm going to go, and I'll come back in a few hours to check on you."

"I'm just going to sit here and look at this thing while you're gone, so you might as well sit with me," Hannah said stubbornly.

"I'm not going to lie…I need a break as much as you need rest. What do you want for dinner? I'll bring you back something, so you won't have to rely on hospital food."

"Surprise me."

"All right. Seriously, try to get a little nap in. I need you one-hundred percent if we are going to finish this hunt properly."

"I'll try, but no promises."

Standing up I moved towards Hannah and kissed her on the forehead before turning to pull the shade on the window.

"Hey." She said. "I was enjoying the view."

"Too bad. Now get some sleep."

I walked out of the room leaving her still with the tablet in hand and headed out to Calhoun Street. The town had woken up considerably since I had walked into the hospital and now traffic was as thick as the mix of college students and tourists on the sidewalk. Weaving through vacationers taking pictures and students texting I managed to make it over to King Street, where I grabbed a sandwich and a beer before heading back to my place. I needed a nap and planned on energizing my batteries.

Unfortunately, my place was not as empty as I had hoped. Waiting for me was Colin sitting on my porch in shorts and a Cleveland Indians t-shirt. Chief Wahoo was grinning at me as I watched Colin wash down a bite of hotdog with his beer.

"I can see you've gone off duty," I said, joining him.

"What can I say, my work was done. I might as well get a little vacation out of this trip. We should rent a charter boat and go fishing."

"Wish I could. Life would be a lot easier. I thought you were getting a hotel room."

"I said I might get one. Your place is in a good spot, and I don't mind the couch."

I knew Colin wasn't getting a room, and honestly, I never expected him too, but I liked to push the issue.

"How's Hannah doing?" He asked.

"Awake and as feisty as ever. I left hoping she would get some rest, but I doubt it."

"What are your plans? I mean is this whole mess over now for you two?"

"Nope, she wants to finish what we started, and I'm kind of for it. I'm not sure why, but there is an urge to understand what all of this was for…the murders, the threats, and even Tidwell's craziness."

"I am officially on vacation now, but if you need any help just ask."

"It would help pay for your room and board," I said.

"Hey, I bought this hotdog from a street vendor and the beer from the package store with my own money."

"You're still using my couch," I said, taking one of his beers from a small cooler he had by his chair.

"Fine, what are you thinking?"

"Find out anything you can about the KGC. I'm sure there's got to be some FBI files or maybe even something at the Southern Poverty Law Center that could help us to get a better understanding of who we're dealing with."

"Are you positive that's who you're up against?"

"No, I'm not positive, but everything has pointed in that direction since Hannah showed me the letter from Trenholm's study.

CHAPTER 73

"Going back to my cross theory," Hannah said, "the one marking the sites on the map and laying the shape of a cross over it."

"I haven't forgotten. You've got 1 Broad Street at the top of the cross and Magnolia Cemetery at the bottom. The school and the wharf make up the other points. So what's your point?"

"My point is, I'm struggling to read the clues on the urn, but we have to assume that the next location is the middle of the cross." She circled a small area on the map she had brought up on her tablet. "I could GPS the exact center of the cross, but I doubt what we are looking for is in the exact center."

"What do you mean?"

"The whole series of clues and the final point were all laid out before GPS first of all, but more importantly each site has held some importance to whoever originally put this all together. They all have some connection to the Trenholms or the South before the war. I believe that there is a combination of symbol and meaning going on with these clues. The cross is a symbol, and the

259

locations have meaning. We are going to be looking for a location near the center of the cross that also holds some significance."

"Seems to make sense, but how do we move forward then?" I watched as Hannah zoomed in on the area of the map using satellite images. "Is it going to be that easy?"

"No, I was just hopeful. Why don't you go for a walk?"

"Excuse me?"

"A walk. Go check out these blocks." Hannah once again pointed to her map. "East Bay north to Mary, west to Meeting, south to Calhoun, and then finally back over to East Bay. Don't just walk on these streets, but get into the neighborhood and really look. Make sure you have your phone and research the area while you're there."

"Haven't you already done that?"

"No, I've been busy working on the urn, and this idea just came to me out of frustration. Give me your phone for a second."

I handed Hannah my phone, and she played with for a moment.

"Here," she pointed at the screen, "I downloaded a tourist app for you. You program in the neighborhood you're in, and it gives you a walking tour. The audio tours are done by local tour guides, but there are also little tidbits written in by the apps users."

"Why do I have to walk around looking like a tourist with my head in my phone?" I definitely was whining a little.

"Because, tour guides make money by stretching the truth and adding a lot of myth or local lore to their tours. It's a good way to stumble upon something that won't be in a library or research database. A lot of it is complete bullshit, but every once in a while, there is some truth behind these stories."

"Basically, you're sending me out to spend my day walking around town, like a tourist, and with my head attached to my phone like an idiot."

"Good, you've got it," Hannah said with a smile. "I'll keep working here and call you if I come up with anything…I know you'll have your phone close."

"Very amusing. I'll be going before you add any more fun to my day."

"All right, stay in touch. And Jack, we've been really lucky so far, but I've got a feeling this won't be so easy."

I walked to the door and began program my new phone app. "She thinks this has been easy," I said under my breath.

"What's that?" Hannah asked.

"I'll be in touch," I said, leaving for my guided tour of Charleston.

CHAPTER 74

Walking around the beautiful city for two hours, listening to polluted facts from a tour guide, and getting a little sun in the process would define a vacation for some people, but for me it was a pain in the ass. I was able to learn a vast amount of worthless information that would never earn me a dime but found nothing that led me to believe I was close to finding a KGC cache. With sore feet and a burnt forehead, I was about ready to give up.

"I'm striking out here," I said into my cell phone. "Have you made any progress?"

"I'm working on a couple things, but nothing substantial yet." Hannah was apparently hitting some brick walls too. "Where are you right now?"

"Walking in front of the library on Calhoun Street. I've got one last block to go over before I give up and find a cold beer."

"What block is that?"

"I don't know. Whatever is between here and East Bay?"

"What's your tour say about that area?" Hannah asked.

"Nothing."

"Are you sure?"

"No. I turned it off. It was pointless and had more information about whores and ghost stories than real information."

"How long ago did you stop listening?"

"Jesus…what's with all the questions?"

"Jack," Hannah said in a firm voice. "When did you turn it off?"

"Just now, before I called you."

Hannah was silent for a moment. "Okay, turn it back on and finish up your little tour. Call me back when you're done."

"Why?"

"Because I think I'm on to something, but I don't want to tell you what it is."

"Why not?" I was a little annoyed.

"Just call me back when you finish." Hannah hung up not giving me a chance to argue further.

I turned my guided tour back on and marched towards the Cooper River. The voice coming from my phone guided me down Alexander Street, a small side street filled with half commercial and half residential houses. Most were asking for some TLC and compared to the rest of the city Alexander Street lacked charm and beauty. The tour guided me to my right where a dilapidated Charleston single house stood. It was fenced in from the neighbors and the street with a black iron fence. There was no yard that I could see looking between two iron bars, instead a black top parking lot with a large tree in the center. According to the tour, the tree was Charleston's Liberty Tree or a replacement for the original that once stood there. Apparently, the tree was the spot where Christopher Gadsden and his Liberty Boys would gather to advocate the colony's independence, and where the Declaration of Independence was first read.

While I listened to the information flowing from my phone, I began to wonder why such a historic site was fenced off from the public, surrounded by blacktop, and attached to a run-down old house. In a city where objects of the slightest historical significance were hoisted on a pedestal and applauded, why was this site off the radar and off limits? My first gut instinct was that the tour guides did not have any historical proof that this was the actual Liberty Tree location, but as I walked the edge of the fence, I came across a plaque from the Sons of the American Revolution marking the spot. The plaque was small, weathered, and turning green in parts but I could make out the information I needed to confirm what my audio tour had said.

I continued to walk the fence line surrounding the property and snapped some photos like Hannah would have. Nothing I came across told me that this was the KGC spot I had been searching for, but my gut told me that there was something not right going on here.

"Hannah," I said into my phone, "what do you know about Charleston's Liberty Tree?"

"I was hoping it would intrigue you." She said. "I didn't want to mention it because I was afraid my opinion would influence you. What made you stop there?"

"My tour, but it's odd."

"Why? What's odd about it?"

"It seems like a really historically significant spot, but no one knows it's here and it's not kept up at all. Most historical locations in this town are monitored, manicured, and mapped for every tourist to see."

"Any KGC markings?" Hannah asked.

"Not that I've seen, but this is the only lead I've seen in the neighborhood, and my gut is telling me there's something here."

"What about the tree?"

"What about it?"

"Are there any markings on or around the tree? Remember the tree in St. Phillip's Cemetery, and the KGC is known for using trees called Wisdom Trees to hide clues."

"The whole property is fenced in, and the tree is standing right in the middle surrounded by an old blacktop parking lot. I can't see anything from where I'm standing."

"Can't you jump the fence?"

"Jump no, but climbing it is a possibility." I looked at the fence line and out to the street. No one was around, but inside the fence I would have no way to hide. "Maybe I should come back tonight."

"Just go now and make it quick," Hannah said. "If you see anything, snap some pictures and get out fast."

"I'm pretty visible here. Someone could see me, and I would be trespassing on private property."

"If you get caught pretend you're a dumb tourist who doesn't know any better."

"All right, but be ready to bail me out."

I glanced around once more and saw no one, so over the fence I began to go.

CHAPTER 75

"What do you think you're doing?" A voice resounded behind me.

I looked behind me and down towards the ground. One of my legs was already over the top of the fence, and at the sound of the voice I had frozen in a peculiar position. Below I could see a blonde woman, dressed in the blues of the Charleston Police Department, and wearing a bike helmet with one strap dangling off to the side. Out on the sidewalk leaning against a light post I could see her police bike.

"I was just trying to get a picture of the Liberty Tree," I said with my best smile.

"You know that's private property, so I suggest you get down before I decide to write a citation."

"Yes, ma'am. I'm sorry." I began to climb down off of the fence. When I got my feet back on the ground, the officer stood with her arms crossed. "I am truly sorry. I only wanted a closer shot, and the property looked abandoned."

I wasn't sure if she believed me as she stood in silence for a moment before finally speaking. "Tourists." She said shaking her head. "Now, get out of here, and stay off of other peoples' property."

"Yes, ma'am," I said again. "And thank you."

Walking off down the sidewalk back towards Calhoun I could feel her eyes staring a hole through my back.

I made my way down Calhoun and wandered through Marion Square while I talked to Hannah on the phone. It worried me that she hadn't deciphered the urn yet because the other clues had come to her so quickly. On the other hand, she did have information on the Liberty Tree that was intriguing. Apparently, the original tree had been cut down, and the stump burned when the British occupied Charleston during the Revolution. After the war, the Sons of Liberty dug up the root structure and used the wood to make a cane that was sent to Thomas Jefferson. Another tree was then planted to replace the one destroyed by the British.

Hannah had also dug up land records for the Alexander Street property that housed the tree. There was no information about it being sold or possession changing hands, but the tax information identified a group called The Charleston Club as the party responsible for the property. Having looked further into The Charleston Club, Hannah found very little except for a few more properties in the city listed through tax records. There was one at 53 East Bay Street that she found particularly fascinating. First, was its location was extremely close to where Jason Trenholm had been killed. The second reason was because of a photo of the property Hannah had found online. It was taken from the front of the house and slightly off to the left of the structure was a gate with a small sign that read *The Charleston Club A.D. 1852*. For both Hannah and me, the founding of the club about the same time as the KGC appeared on the scene was no coincidence.

We both knew that I had to get a closer look at that Liberty Tree, but I wasn't sure how. Even if I went over the fence at night someone could easily see me because of the openness of the parking lot around the tree and the light coming from the street lamps. I also needed to get in touch with Colin and see if he had come up with any further information that may come in useful. Colin might still be in law enforcement, but I also had a hunch he might know of a way to get a little closer to that tree.

After hanging up with Hannah, I called Colin and made plans to meet him for a drink and a bite to eat. Finally getting off of the phone, I realized that Marion Square was filled with beautiful college girls sunning themselves while the men tossed Frisbees and kicked soccer balls around a towering monument to John C. Calhoun. What a life. Had I gone to college here I would have never left. Heading towards King Street, I finally made it across the square straining my neck only slightly from staring at all the bikini-clad coeds. At the corner of King and Calhoun, a black SUV pulled up in front of me and the window rolled down revealing two men wearing suits and sunglasses. My first thought was that they were Feds, but the suits were too tailored.

"Get in." The one in the passenger seat said as he used his thumb to point towards the back.

"I'd rather not."

The man in the passenger seat lifted his jacket flap slightly to reveal a Glock in its holster. "Get in." He said again.

"Sorry, I'm going to have to pass."

The two men looked at each other as the car behind them honked its horn. I could see that they were both making moves to get out of the car, and I was seriously considering running.

"Is there a problem here gentlemen?" A voice like an angel came from behind me.

"No problem officer." The man in the passenger seat said.

"Great, then get moving you're blocking traffic."

Without another word, the SUV drove off, and I turned to see a blonde policewoman on her bike. It was the same one that had just chased me off of the Liberty Tree property.

"I don't know what your deal is," she said, "but I don't want to have to run into you again today."

"No ma'am," I said as she pedaled off down King Street.

I wasn't sure what she had just saved me from, but I knew that I should probably be thankful.

CHAPTER 76

"Who do you think they were?" Colin asked me.

"Not sure, but I believe some kind of private security."

We were sitting at the bar at CO stuffing our faces with curried noodles and kimchi beef dumplings. There were only two other people at the other end of the bar, so we had some freedom to talk.

"Does Trenholm have a security team?" Colin asked.

"Not that I know of. If it was Trenholm, I think he would have simply sent Makem again. Someone else has gotten involved or else I'm completely missing something."

"Tidwell is out of the picture, so doesn't that only leave Trenholm?"

"Not necessarily. I have no idea if the KGC and The Charleston Club are one and the same, but even if they're not each would have plenty of members to support Trenholm."

"If Trenholm is any indication of the membership then the rest of the members must have some pretty powerful sway too."

Colin had a point, but what had I done to attract new attention? If anything, we should have been off the radar a little bit after the events at Tidwell's plantation and Trenholm recovering the urn.

"I still need to figure out how to get a closer look at that tree."

"Telescopic lens," Colin said. "You might not be able to get every detail, but you'll sure as hell be able to see if anything is carved on that tree trunk."

"Not a bad idea. Do you want to take care of that for me?"

"Why?"

"There's a bike cop in that neighborhood who kind of has my number."

"All right, but this is really starting to cut into my vacation. By the way, my search for the KGC turned out to be a dead end. The FBI didn't exist during their heyday, so we don't have any records, and the government's official status for them is that they disbanded in 1916. The Southern Poverty Law Center isn't tracking them as a hate group because they don't officially exist, so I've got nothing."

"I'm not surprised, but it was worth a shot."

Colin was staring out the window of the restaurant, and I thought he was watching a group of college girls window shop, but he hadn't been.

"You don't believe that the two men in the SUV were the same two that took a shot at you and Hannah from the boat?"

"I actually hadn't thought of that, but they could have been. I didn't get a good look at either of them while hanging from the rocks."

"Maybe they aren't a security team, but hired thugs."

I thought about this for a moment. "Trenholm has his personal muscle in Makem and then hires out corporate muscle for situations that are slightly more delicate, or because he has a known relationship to Makem he uses these two guys for more subtle matters."

"It makes sense. We know Trenholm has his hands spread out all over the place so he would need help, and Makem isn't exactly polished in getting things done quietly."

"That actually worries me more. If Trenholm has stopped sending Makem to deal with me, then everything just got really grave."

"Hannah may be right," Colin said. "There may be more here than lost Confederate gold."

CHAPTER 76

I was honestly perplexed. My mind couldn't grasp what was so important that it needed to be so well hidden, and I wasn't talking about any gold left over from the Confederacy. The gold now appeared to be only a symbol of a deeper secret, and I was stumped as to what that was. Hannah was having no better luck trying to unlock the clues of the urn, and she was becoming increasingly frustrated. It didn't help that she felt captive in her hospital room. The doctor was holding on to her for a few more days, but I feared she would break herself out at any moment.

Relying on Colin to continue looking into the Liberty Tree location, I now had time on my hands but no idea what to do with it. There was no way I was going to stay out of sight or continuously looking over my shoulder for whatever muscle Trenholm was going to throw my way, so I decided to go for a walk with my morning coffee.

Wandering aimlessly often brings you to places that you intended to go all along or a place that your subconscious knew you needed to go. I found myself walking the Battery and staring out across the water to Fort Sumter. Only half the size of its former self, the island fort was a representation of the whole Confederacy, the ugly war that followed, and the destruction it brought to the South. From where I stood I could picture the guns firing on the fort. The constant bombardment slowly breaking its thick walls into rubble, as chaos ruled those trapped inside. The city of Charleston was no different than the fort, having suffered through constant bombardment during the war too, and for what…it had to be more than just slavery.

I looked around. My surroundings were beautiful, flowers in full bloom, massive oaks dripping with Spanish moss, and luxurious homes overlooking the park and harbor. No, the Southerners didn't start a war over just slavery. Slavery was a symbol. To the South, it was a symbol of a way of life that was being threatened. A right to govern and rule themselves, to keep a promise of government for the people by the people. They feared that the North had taken hold of the Federal Government and that the South would be engulfed by the northern industrial machine. For the North, and for Lincoln, slavery was a symbol to be used for propaganda. It was used to position the Union on the side of good and the South as evil. It is the oldest story ever told, good versus evil, and slavery was a way for the North to sell that story to the world. In the end, both the North and the South came out of the war stronger than ever, tied together as one nation, and yet the purpose of the war, those slaves, were quickly tossed to the side and returned their less than human status.

Moving on down the sea wall and into the neighborhood along Waterfront Park, I continued to try and piece together Trenholm's motivation. Tidwell's reasons were obvious. He was a deranged man haunted by his family's dishonor. Simple revenge is often the easiest motivation. Trenholm was different, or was it also pure revenge? Could someone still be that bitter towards the North, for losing a war fought over a lost cause, and the Reconstruction that followed? Were Trenholm and his cohorts only pissed that the Civil War and Reconstruction had halted the South's march towards a permanent aristocratic life? I looked around at my surroundings once again, canopies of lush green, multimillion dollar homes, and streets lined with luxury cars.

Somehow I couldn't imagine them doing much better than they already were, so why the animosity? Why still have the KGC?

The steeple of St. Phillip's was poking its head out over the trees and the buildings along East Bay Street, and it called to me as I ventured away from the water and down Queen Street. As I felt my body being pulled towards the church, I watched the people on the streets. There was a significant difference between how the tourists and the locals behaved. It wasn't because one group was always taking pictures, but instead in the way they carried themselves. The locals had a confidence to them that was different and actually distinct. What made these people separate from the rest of the world? What made them so unique in a country filled with individuals? Is it that the South takes its strength from their memory, loyalty to family, to ancestors that sacrificed so much for the Southern cause, and in the end, their honor is exemplified through their own self-worth and complemented by those around them?

Before I realized it, I found myself standing in front of the Calhoun monument in the eastern portion of St. Phillip's Cemetery. Once again, I looked at my surroundings. The grass that needed to be trimmed around broken stones was in sharp contrast to the family plots so well-manicured it seemed they were looked after on a daily basis. I could see the James family graves and the wisdom tree that started my trek through this ancient city. Suddenly, I found myself reading and rereading the bible quote at the bottom of Calhoun's memorial, James 3. My mind clicked, and I remember the quote from Isaiah that we had also found. Neither Hannah nor I had followed up on these verses having been so caught up in our little treasure hunt. What if we had missed something from the very beginning, something huge? It was time to re-evaluate what we were doing.

CHAPTER 77

"I don't know," Hannah said. "They just seem like words of wisdom to me."

I read over the three pieces of scripture we were looking at. James 3:1-5 was obvious, but we still weren't sure whether we needed to be looking at Isaiah 8:12 or Isaiah 44:12.

"What's the distinctions between the two verses of Isaiah?" I asked her.

"Okay, Isaiah 8:12 is about conspiracy. The people considered Isaiah a traitor because he said that Ahaz and his administration were wrong to rely on Assyria."

"So the verse uses the word confederacy for conspiracy?"

"Correct."

"I still think this has to be it. The KGC were loyal to the confederacy and were hatching a conspiracy against the Union." I read the verse again. "Say ye not, A confederacy, to all them to whom this people shall say, A confederacy; neither fear ye their fear, nor be afraid."

"Maybe, but Isaiah 44:12 basically translates to; an idol may be a work of art. But even the finest craftsman's mortality is revealed in his hunger and thirst. Couldn't the idol be the Federal Government, held up in such high regard because of the success of the nation in the years after the Civil War? At the turn of the century, the country became an industrial giant, overcame the depression and fascism, and eventually a superpower. Is it too hard to think that we hold America up in a false light and that we often forget about its mortality? To me, this verse has the KGC written all over it."

"It does make sense. But what does it mean in correlation to the verse on Calhoun's memorial, James 3:1-5?"

"Let's see." Hannah thought for a moment and then studied her tablet. "It seems that the verses in the Book of James have a theme of humility, and basically tells us that you can control your actions by controlling your tongue. Therefore, one should work on one's speech as much as other areas of behavior."

"I'm not seeing a connection."

"Neither am I," Hannah said.

"Maybe they are both telling us that we need to learn humility, it is something that all Americans could use a little more of."

"Could be, but if these are clues then to where?"

"There's something else. If these are clues then what were all those clues we were following before?"

Hannah breathed out loudly. "I told you before that the KGC system was intricate. They've been known to put out false trails that lead people in an entirely different direction than where they want to go."

"So maybe that's what these verses are. Why else would Makem have been so eager to get his hands on that urn?"

"To lead us to believe that we were on the right path."

"It's depressing to think you might be right."

A knock came at the door of Hannah's hospital room, and Colin walked in.

"What are you two up to?" He asked.

"Dead end after dead end. Did you find anything at the Liberty Tree today?" I asked.

"Dead end as well."

"Are you sure?" Hannah asked, seemingly rejected.

"Positive. I looked at that tree from every angle I could. The lens worked so well I could see an ant climbing on a piece of bark, so trust me there weren't any carvings."

"It was worth a shot," I said. "Now we are left with either deciphering the urn or turning two bible verses into clues…if we're going to get anywhere."

"I'm going back to the house," Colin said.

"Holdup, I'll go with you. I think Hannah and I've both had enough for one day."

"I agree, my brain is fried. Jack, can you be back here at eleven tomorrow morning?"

"Sure, why?"

"I'm getting out of this place, and I'll need you to carry my bag."

"I thought the doctor was making you stay a little longer. You're not breaking out, are you?" I thought it prudent to ask.

"I brokered a deal with him. Now be on time. I can't take another minute of this place."

CHAPTER 78

With Hannah a free woman again, we began to pour our time into trying to decipher the hidden message in the Bible verses and the code on the urn. My biggest fear was that neither route had anything to actually decrypt. For two straight days, we were holed up at my place as we watched Colin come and go from the beach and the golf course. I was jealous and frustrated. Part of me wanted to throw it all away and join him for an afternoon sipping beers at a bar on Folly Beach. Hannah was my motivation, as long as she was still in...then so was I.

We had dinner at FIG, and afterward, Colin headed off to find a sports bar that would show the Indians game. Hannah and I went south on Meeting Street and back towards my place for some more work. At the corner of Meeting and Cumberland, we heard the sound of a car slowing down behind us, and a curious glance over my shoulder was all I needed to see it was the same SUV that had stopped me near Marion Square the other day.

"Speed up," I said to Hannah, under my breath as we turned down Cumberland.

I could hear car doors close behind us and the sound of footsteps coming in our directions. The soles of dress shoes make a distinct sound, and they clicked off of the cement as the pace quickened from whoever was behind us.

Hannah made a subtle look behind her to see what I already knew. "Two men, two suits, and they're coming up fast."

It had to be Tweedle-Dee and Tweedle-Dum from the other day.

"All right, on the count of three we take off. Can you run with your leg?"

"I'll be fine," Hannah said.

"Make a bee-line for the nearest public spot. One, two three."

We took off running, and I was surprised by Hannah's quickness. She had recovered from her gunshot wound well. The moment we started moving, I could hear the two behind us do the same thing, but there was another distinct sound that I heard. One of them was talking into a radio as he ran.

Hannah was outpacing me, and it was a good thing. I wanted to stay in between her and our pursuers. She sprinted down Cumberland and crossed over the intersection of Church with me about ten feet behind her. I wondered why she didn't turn on Church and head towards the Market, a place always full of people, but instead it looked like she was going to the busy restaurant district of East Bay Street.

At full go, Hannah sprinted down the south side of Cumberland. I followed, occasionally looking over my shoulder at the two behind us. They weren't gaining, but they were still there. Suddenly, I looked up, and Hannah was gone. Somehow she vanished in the time it took me to turn my head. I hadn't realized where she had gone until I almost passed by the entrance.

Philadelphia Alley connected Cumberland with Queen Street and ran behind the St. Phillip's Church grounds. The light at its entrance had been out, which is the reason I missed Hannah make the turn, maybe she thought our pursuers wouldn't see either.

At the moment it took me to acknowledge the alley entrance and realize that's where Hannah went, I lost ground to the two men behind us. They were close now and weren't going to be fooled by my sudden turn down the alleyway. I could hear one of them on the radio again, but it didn't concern me. All I cared about was reaching the end of the alley and getting back out in the open again.

The cobblestone path wasn't the best surface to run on, and I watched Hannah struggle in front of me a few times. The pack was beginning to bunch up. I was gaining on Hannah and the two men were gaining on me. Up ahead I could see Queen Street through the darkness, and Hannah was almost there. We pressed on and right as Hannah was about to turn onto the street she caught herself on a rounded edge of a cobblestone. Her ankle twisted and I could see her go down hard. Before I could even react a black SUV pulled up on Queen Street and blocked our exit from the alley. Two more men got out, picked Hannah up from the ground and pushed her inside the back of the vehicle. I was certain they were going to take off with her, but instead, they stood there waiting for me.

There was no place to fight what was about to happen, so I slowed my pace to a walk and got into the back of the SUV willingly to join Hannah. Hoods were placed on both of our heads as the sounds of the engine told me we were on the move.

CHAPTER 79

We were rustled from the vehicle with hoods on and led through a building of some sort. From the sounds made by our shoes, I gathered the floors were hardwood, and the echoes told me the space was large. Guided down a flight of stairs, I could feel the damp air of a cellar. Soon, two hands pushed down on my shoulders as I was forced into a stiff wooden chair. The hoods stayed on, and I could hear the sounds of our captures departing.

"Hannah," I said. "Are you all right?"

"I'm fine. Twisted my ankle a bit, but I'll survive. Where do you think they've taken us?"

"No idea. It seemed like we were in the car for at least a half-hour, but that could have been done on purpose."

"What do you mean?"

"They might have been driving around longer then they needed to so we wouldn't be able to figure out where we were going."

I could hear the door open from above and the sound of voices came to me in a mumbled form. Footsteps, more than just two men, made their way across the floor above us.

"We've got company," I said to Hannah.

"Yeah, but who?"

The door to the cellar opened, and the sounds of footsteps began their march towards us almost in unison. From the darkness of my hood, I could tell lights had been turned on around us, bright lights…interrogation style.

The hoods came off, and the light was immediately blinding. When my eyes began to adjust, I could see two of our captures off to either side of Hannah and I. From what I could tell they were the same duo that had stopped me in Marion Square.

"What's the meaning of this?" I asked the one to my left, but he stood there ice cold.

A voice came from directly in front of us, but the lights kept me from seeing the figure.

"Mr. Francis, it seems you and your little friend here have been poking around in things that are none of your business. I've been told you've repeatedly been warned, but from what information I have on you it seems like you're the stubborn type. A good trait in an investigator, but it often leads you to have issues with authority. I believe that's why you were never cut out for Bureau life."

The figure stepped from the light, and I could now see a face. I knew this man, not personally, but I knew him. He wore a navy blue suit, light blue tie, and had an American Flag pin on his lapel. His polished brown shoes sparkled in the light, but not as much as a large ring on his finger. It was a Citadel ring, just like the one Tommy Makem wore.

"Deputy-Director Bennett," I said to the man in front of me. "Whatever are you doing here?"

James Bennett was a thirty-five year veteran of the FBI. He had been Deputy-Director for the past fifteen and survived three Directors and two Presidents above him. The Citadel ring was all the connection I needed, but I was pretty sure Bennett was a South Carolinian born and raised.

"I was asked to make an appearance on behalf of a dear old friend. It seems that you have become a nuisance and my assistance was needed." The Deputy-Director said.

"A dear old friend?" I was pretty sure who he meant.

As if on cue, George Trenholm stepped from the shadows to join Deputy-Director Bennett in front of Hannah and me.

"Hello, Jack," Trenholm said. "And this must be the professor that my son enjoyed so much."

Hannah smiled, but not with pleasure. It looked more like she was ready to spit in the man's face.

"Now, what to do with these two?" Trenholm said, turning towards Bennett.

CHAPTER 80

They left us to ourselves for quite some time. We were both still tied to our chairs and the lamps shone brightly in our faces. My forehead was beginning to sweat from their heat. Hannah and I talked very little, and I was starting to worry about her more than myself. Life is simpler when you only have yourself to worry about, but once you start to feel responsible for someone else, it takes on a whole other level of complexity.

"They don't know what to do with us," I said to Hannah.

All I got was a small grunt in response. The poor woman had been through a lot and all for a research project. When I started my career, I knew that I would be putting myself in danger, but I don't think that's on most people's minds when they choose the life of a college professor.

The delay and the wait had me thinking. Our captors didn't quite know what to do with us. In most cases, we probably would have just disappeared, but it was not that easy. Hannah would be missed and her connection to the Trenholms, through Jason, was too apparent. I had an FBI Agent looking out for me, and even though the Deputy-Director could probably silence Colin he would cause a lot of trouble along the way. So, where did that leave them?

It was at least two hours, maybe more, before I heard footsteps coming from above and then the cellar door opened. The two goons lead the way followed by Deputy-Director Bennett, Trenholm, and a new figure…Professor Thompson.

The old college professor looked at Hannah and me and shook his head as if getting ready to scold us. He no longer seemed like the sweet Southern gentleman I had met at his Tradd Street residence, but instead a man bitter with disappointment.

"I never dreamed it would come to this," Thompson said in his South of Broad drawl. "Mr. Bennett and Mr. Trenholm seem to be at a loss trying to decide what to do with you two. Mr. Trenholm, I afraid, never wants to see you again, but some of us realize that if you simply disappeared it would only cause more problems. My opinion is to try and bring the both of you to your senses, and then maybe we can all return to our lives. I understand Professor Welsh's need to find answers, but Mr. Francis what is your stake in all of this? Are you out to make a name for yourself?"

"I only want to know the truth. What is so important that your son had to die over it?" I asked looking at Trenholm.

"The truth?" Thompson asked. He was silent for a second thinking about his next words carefully. "All right, I'll give you the truth. This country works because there are different people with different beliefs, and not because we are all the same." Thompson began. "The South is a genuinely different place, unique, and beautiful despite and because of our history. What you're digging up is the past, and a part of that past causes a lot of people pain in all parts of our nation."

"What we are digging up is the truth. How is that bad?" I asked.

"History is not always about what the truth is, but instead on how we want to remember it," Thompson continued. "What you're digging up could change how people view history. It would change people's perception of the South and cause a reaction that no one in this room could fully comprehend. Let's for a moment say you found a stockpile of hidden Confederate treasure, protected by a secret group with members in all walks of life. These members hold powerful places in our community and our government. I'm not talking here in the South but all across this country. What if this nation thought that these men were hiding large sums of money to one day retake up the Confederate Cause? It would send shockwaves of distrust throughout our society. Let me tell you that nobody wants that, so it's important that what was done in the past does not come back to haunt our future."

"What you telling me is that you're simply protecting a secret to save the solidarity of the Union?" I asked suspiciously.

"Yes."

"I don't believe it. If there is one thing I've learned since coming to Charleston is that beliefs aren't quickly forgotten. There has to be more to it." I said.

"Mr. Francis, look at our country right now. The industrial North is collapsing. Cities that were once the pride of this nation are now desolate and bankrupt. People every day are migrating to the South in large numbers. Here our cities grow strong with new and healthy industry. Our goal is not to have the South rise again...the South has already risen. Did you think for one second that we would take up arms in this day and age? No, the battle for dominance is done through politics and economic engines. The best and brightest from the South look forward to staying home and nurturing their talents, and the cream of the crop from the North are now running to the opportunities we can provide them. Why would we want to shatter appearances by exposing a hundred and fifty-year-old secret?"

I thought about what Thompson said, and he was right. Once mighty cities like Detroit, Cleveland, and Pittsburgh were half of what they used to be. The industry that had won the war for the North was no longer there. Instead, empty factories rotted away, and the population grew smaller. The South had never relied on industrial jobs, so they were in a position to carry on when the North took the hit. How many people did I know that had relocated to cities like Charlotte, Atlanta, and Austin? The South had risen again without anyone really noticing it, and now these men in front of me were greatly profiting from it. They controlled the infrastructure; education, tourism, and banking.

"What then?" I asked. "You want us to simply forget everything we know and move on?"

"You can't live in the past, Mr. Francis." George Trenholm said.

I looked at Hannah, and she looked back to me with an expression that told me she was tired and didn't quite know what to do.

"What about Hannah's work?" I asked Thompson. "What is she supposed to do?"

"Each has its lesson; for our dreams in sooth, come they in shape of demons, gods, or elves, are allegories with deep hearts of truth that tell us solemn secrets of ourselves," Thompson said.

"What is that cryptic nonsense?" I asked.

"Henry Timrod," Hannah answered for me. "He was a famous poet from Charleston and the voice of the South during the Civil War."

"Superb, Professor Welsh," Thompson said. "Now do we all have an understanding?"

I looked to Hannah again, and I knew the answer. "We'll forget everything. No one needs to get hurt, and your lives can all return to normal."

Thompson looked pleased, so did Deputy-Director Bennett, but Trenholm still had an unsettled expression on his face. Something told me that if the truth was ever exposed, he might have the most to lose.

"Trenholm, you don't look happy. Are you going to be able to put this all behind you?" I asked him, with a smug look on my own face.

"Just stay out of my way Francis." The man sulked off back up the stairs.

Deputy-Director Bennett nodded to his two goons and they untied us from our chairs. Thompson and Bennett turned to make their way back up the stairs as I felt the ties on my hands loosen, and then the darkness came as a black hood once again covered my head.

CHAPTER 81

I hate the unfinished, the unknown, and also giving into men that I despised. However, when the two goons dropped Hannah and me off in front of Mrs. Legare's house, I knew it was over. The old woman sat on her lower piazza watching us get out of the back of the black SUV with a look I had never seen before. Something on her face told me that she knew everything, and had sided with Trenholm and the rest of his cronies. Maybe they were right. Maybe some things were best left where they lie.

Hannah had been quiet the whole ride back and her face expressionless. There was no way of telling how she felt about the whole experience. The poor woman had now been kidnapped twice and shot once, and for what? Jason's death and sitting with an upset Bryce the day after his wedding were long in the past. Jason's murder would forever go unsolved, and Bryce would move on to his happy life with his new wife. He would get entrenched in the Charleston lifestyle through his new matrimonial connection, and yet never know the truth about the social class he was joining into.

We made it passed Mrs. Legare with a simple wave and went straight up into the carriage house. Hannah plopped down on the couch and immediately pulled out her tablet. I was actually surprised that Bennett and his muscle hadn't taken it from her. In the kitchen, I grabbed two glasses and a bottle of brown and poured a generous dose of bourbon for Hannah and myself. She still hadn't said a word, and I was beginning to worry. I cradled my glass in my hand, slowly taking the occasional sip, and waited for the woman across from me to break her silence.

"What do they expect from me?" Hannah finally broke her silence after nearly ten minutes. "I should be fearful for my life and thankful I still have it, and yet I can't stop pouring over the research we've collected."

"It's time to let it go," I said, calmly.

"I know. Perhaps I'll put everything away, save everything I have, and come back to it years down the road."

"Probably best."

"You know they're right," Hannah said, as she put down the tablet and reached for her bourbon.

"About what?"

"Everything. The state the country currently finds itself in. The burgeoning new South. I think we both know that finding the remains of the Confederate Treasury would unearth more than gold and silver. The South is barely coming to terms with its slave history, and that took too long. What would a modern conspiracy against the Union do to the fragile social relations of our nation? We, as a people, have become overly sensitive and therefore we may need to be protected from ourselves every once in a while."

"So that's the lesson I'm supposed to learn here? Americans are fragile and need to be protected from themselves. I don't believe it one bit."

"I think the lesson is to not let a society become as easily offended as we have become. Then the truth will have a better chance of surviving."

We sat for a moment in silence, and I topped off our drinks.

"Are you going to keep all that then?" I asked, pointing to her tablet.

"I think I will. Times change you know."

"They do."

I picked up my phone, and a moment later I could hear a sound come from the tablet on the coffee table.

"What's that?" Hannah asked.

"I just sent you everything I had collected, some photos and records."

"Oh, thanks. What now?"

"What now? How about dinner? I'm starving."

EPILOGUE

A few days later I was packing for my return to Cleveland. Mrs. Legare had been less friendly with me since the run in with Mr. Trenholm and Deputy-Director Bennett, so I took it as a sign that I had officially worn out my welcome in Charleston. Hannah had been scarce over the last few days, and I assumed it was because she also knew that it was time for the two of us to go our separate ways. Instead, it was as it had always been…I was on my own, except, of course, for Colin.

Colin was flying back with me and was determined to drink every last beer I had in the carriage house before we left. He was packed and relaxing on the front porch with a cold one, where I had a feeling he would stay until our early morning flight. The tales of his boss' involvement had startled him a little, and he was now keeping a lower profile.

I could hear my phone vibrating on the kitchen counter, and when I reached it, I could see that I had just missed a call from Hannah. *One last goodbye*, I thought. On the call back it rang three times before she picked up.

"Jack, are you still in town?"

"Yeah, until tomorrow morning. Why?"

"I need to see you." She sounded a tad desperate.

"I was going to say goodbye."

"I didn't call you to say goodbye. Any chance you can come meet me?"

"Sure, where?"

"Magnolia Cemetery. The pyramid mausoleum, remember?"

"Sure do. I'll be there in fifteen."

I hung up with Hannah and called out to Colin that I was taking off for a bit. He didn't seem concerned. When the cab dropped me off, I could see Hannah leaning against a car a few yards from the pyramid structure. The urn was still missing from its front entrance, but I noticed that Hannah didn't seem to care. She looked excited and a bit anxious.

"Remember taking pictures of the mausoleum with your phone?" She asked as I approached.

"Yeah, why?"

"Over the past few days, I've been going over everything we collected in our search, including what you sent me the other day."

"I thought you were going to put that away and forget about it for a while," I said.

"I will. Anyways, your pictures, the ones from the backside, revealed something I hadn't seen before."

"What's that?"

"The stained glass window."

"I told you about it," I said. "Explained it in detail, at least I thought I did."

"But you left out something, something I saw in the pictures and was revealed to be important by Professor Thompson the other day."

"Out with it then."

"The words *Rhymed Intro* and *Carolina*."

"Sounds like something out of a poem."

"Exactly," Hannah said. "*Carolina* was a poem by Henry Timrod, the same poet Thompson quoted. And better yet, *Rhymed Intro* is an anagram for Henry Timrod. I believe this was the real clue here. That's why I couldn't decipher the urn." Hannah brought out her trusty tablet and showed me an image of the urn, now with markings highlighted. "*Carolina* was a poem about the great Southern patriots throughout the history of the state. It spoke of heroes of the Revolution and Civil War." Hannah pointed with her finger to the shape of a square, an obelisk, the scales of justice, a cross, and the palmetto moon that represented the State of South Carolina. "There is only one place where these all come together, including Henry Timrod, and it's a place that honors the same type of men spoken of in the poem."

"Where's that?" I asked.

"Washington Square. Now get in the car so we can have a look for ourselves."

My first response was not to go to Washington Square with Hannah. I had made a promise to keep my nose out of other's business, and I had the feeling I was being watched until I left on that plane tomorrow. Somehow, though, in my gut, I knew that this was it…a real ending.

We parked in a metered spot near the corners of Broad and Meeting Street. The locals call the intersection The Four Corners of Law. On one corner sits the law of God with St. Michael's Church. The other three corners house man's law at the federal, state, and local levels. Behind the beautiful city hall building, on the northeast corner is Washington Square.

In the middle of the square was a large obelisk dedicated to the Washington Light Infantry and is adorned with significant military battles. The western entrance is guarded by a statue of President George Washington, and the southern gate by a bust of Henry Timrod.

"The poet is almost on par with the country's greatest leader," I said to Hannah, as we sat on a bench beneath a vast shadowy oak.

"That's not all. On the back wall is a memorial to General Pierre Beauregard, defender of the city during the Civil War. That same wall houses dedications to those lost, Masonic plaques, and even memorials from the Society of Cincinnatus. The north entrance has a commemoration to Andre Jackson's mother, a native, and in the middle of it all the ultimate marker, an obelisk."

"What does it all mean?" I asked.

"The square has been here since 1818, but all of this…the memorials, statues, and markers…were added after the Civil War. The two essential pieces, the obelisk and the Henry Timrod bust, were added in 1891 and 1901 respectively."

298

"What you're saying is that this whole square was designed to honor the heroes of South Carolina? Well, that doesn't seem so odd."

"It wouldn't, except for the clues that point here and the fact that the obelisk was donated by James Trenholm, son of the Confederate Treasure and ancestor to Jason Trenholm."

"Are you saying that the remains of the Confederate Treasury are under the obelisk?"

"I'm sure that whatever treasure the Trenholm's were hiding is buried here. It's too perfect. What I wouldn't give for a few metal detectors and some ground image software."

"I'm not sold," I said, standing to have a better look around.

I began to walk. The dedications to Andrew Jackson's mother and General Beauregard were short and sweet. Henry Timrod's bust held a vague description of the man, and the George Washington statue filled me with American pride. I circled around the obelisk on the brick path. The sun trickled in through the tree branches as I moved. There were tourists around, but I felt alone in the park, a cool reprieve from the Carolina heat. Names of battlefields graced the steps that led up to the column, and I mouthed the name of each one as I walked around.

"Manassas, Fort Sumter, Secessionville." I read to myself quietly, as I moved around the circle surrounding the memorial.

Kneeling down behind the Washington statue, I could see a direct line from my point through the obelisk and to the Beauregard Memorial. I walked around and knelt behind Henry Timrod's bust, and I had the same direct line to Elizabeth Jackson's marker. The square was laid out perfectly symmetrical with each significant marker…the exact same distance apart and forming a perfect cross, or from another angle an x. I could see Hannah watching me and she was smiling. Closer, I walked towards the obelisk, and I traversed the grass barrier from the brick path to the first step. It was there, above the words *Fort Sumter*, that I saw my answer. The hooked x was only slightly visible, etched softly into the marble step, but it was undeniably there. I looked at Hannah, who was now moving towards me with a smile of satisfaction on her face.

"X marks the spot," I said to her.

"You might say that."

Other Titles by
MP Murphy

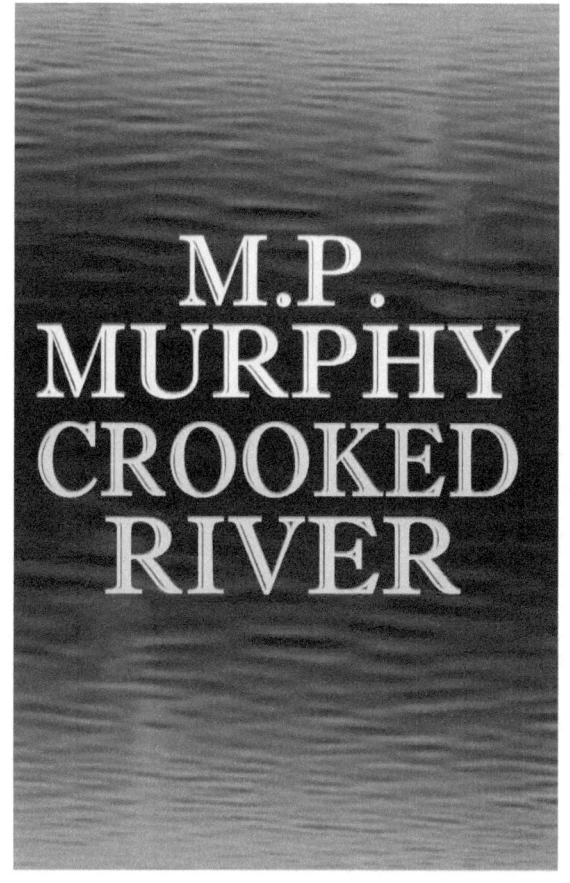

A Jack Francis Novel

And…..

Killing Floor:
Memoir of a Serial Killer

MP Murphy

Available on Amazon.com and in the Kindle Library